Penguin Modern Classics
Peter Camenzind

Hermann Hesse was born at Calw, Germany, on 2 July 1877.
Having begun his career as a bookseller in Tübingen and
Basle, he started to write and to publish poetry at the age of
twenty-one. Five years later he enjoyed his first major
success with his novels on youth and educational problems:
first *Peter Camenzind*, then *Unterm Rad* (*The Prodigy*),
followed by *Gertrud*, *Rosshalde*, *Demian*, and others.
Later, when as a protest against German militarism in the
First World War he settled permanently in Switzerland, he
established himself as one of the greatest literary figures
of the German-speaking world. His humanity, his searching
philosophy developed further in such novels as *Der
Steppenwolf* and *Narziss und Goldmund*, while his poems and
critical writings won him a leading place among
contemporary thinkers. The Nazis abhorred and
suppressed his books; the Swiss honoured him by conferring
on him the degree of Ph.D.; the world paid homage to him,
finally, by bestowing upon him in 1946 the Nobel Prize
for Literature, an award richly deserved by his great novel
Das Glasperlenspiel (*The Glass Bead Game*). Hermann
Hesse died in 1962, shortly after his eighty-fifth birthday.

Hermann Hesse

Peter Camenzind

Translated from the German
by W. J. Strachan

Penguin Books

Penguin Books Ltd, Harmondsworth,
Middlesex, England
Penguin Books Australia Ltd, Ringwood,
Victoria, Australia

Peter Camenzind first published 1904
This translation first published by Peter Owen, 1961
Published in Penguin Books, 1973

Copyright © Hermann Hesse, 1953
This translation copyright © Peter Owen Ltd, 1961

Made and printed in Great Britain by
Hunt Barnard Printing Ltd, Aylesbury, Bucks.
Set in Monotype Plantin

Chapter One

In the beginning was the myth. Just as Almighty God once conveyed his message through the souls of Hindoos, Greeks and Teutons, he continues to express his love every day in the soul of every child.

At that time in my life I did not know the names of the lake, mountains and streams of my native place. But I saw the smooth blue-green water sparkling with tiny lights in the sunshine and, in a close girdle around it, the steep mountains whose gulleys were filled with glistening snow in their topmost heights, tiny waterfalls, and at the foot, the bright, sloping meadows, peopled with orchards and grey Alpine cattle. And as my poor little heart was so blank and quiet, full of expectancy, the spirits of the lake and mountains inscribed their fine and stirring deeds upon it. The stubborn cliffs and precipices spoke to it in tones of awe and defiance of times whose sons they are and whose scars they bear. They spoke of the past when the earth with moans of pain heaved and burst asunder and squeezed the mountain peaks and crests out of her tortured womb. Walls of rock surged up, rumbling and cracking to split aimlessly into mountain tops; twin summits fought desperately for space until one would soar triumphant, shattering and deposing its brother. Here and there, several crags that went back to those days were suspended high up in the fissures, rocky walls, split apart and disrupted; and, with every thaw, gushing water swept down great boulders as huge as houses, shivered them like glass or bore them down irresistibly into the deep, gentle meadows below.

Those craggy mountains always related the same story. And when one saw their precipitous walls with layers of rock, cleft, twisted or reft asunder, each filled with gaping wounds, it was easy to understand them. 'We have suffered indescribable horrors,' they said, 'and we are suffering still.' But their voices were proud and stern, and they spoke with the restraint of old, indomitable warriors.

Warriors indeed. I saw them do battle against water and storm in the grim nights of early Spring when the enraged *Föhn* roared round their hoary heads and the rushing torrents tore new, raw pieces from their flanks. There they stood in those nights with their obstinately clinging roots – dark, breathless, sullen – confronting the storm with their cleft walls and summits, and gathered all their strength as they crowded defiantly together. And with every wound they received one could hear their terrible roar of rage and fear, and even through the distant landslides their terrible moans re-echoed, broken and angry.

And I saw meadows and slopes and earth-filled crevices, covered with grasses, flowers, bracken and mosses to which the ancient dialect of the place had given strange evocative names. Children and grandchildren of the mountains, they remained coloured and unconcerned. I felt them, examined them, smelt their scent and learned their names. The sight of the trees affected me more seriously and more deeply. I watched each with its independent life, forming its own particular shape, casting its own individual shadow. Settlers and warriors, they seemed to have a closer relationship with the mountains, especially those which stood higher on the mountain, for each had to maintain its hard, silent struggle for existence and growth against wind, weather and rock. Each had to bear its burden, cling firmly, thereby gaining its individual aspect and particular scars. There were Scotch pines whose growth of branches storms had restricted to one side and trees whose red trunks had twisted themselves like snakes round overhanging rocks, so that tree and rock pressed and clung together in a tight embrace. They gazed at me like soldiers and inspired awe and respect in my heart.

Our men and women resembled them; they were hard,

close-knit, niggard of speech – the best of them, the more so. Hence I learned to look upon men as upon trees and rocks, to think about them, to honour and to love them just as I loved the quiet pines.

Our small village of Nimikon lies by the lake on a triangular slope, hemmed in on either side by two rocky spurs. One path leads to a near by monastery, a second to a neighbouring hamlet, four and a half hours' walk away. The other villages, bordering the lake, are reached by boat. Our houses are built in the old timber-frame style and have no particular age; new buildings are seldom constructed, and the old cottages are repaired piecemeal, as required – one year the floor, another a section of the roof. Many half-beams and planks, which previously belonged to the wall, now function as joists and when they cannot serve this purpose and are too good for firewood, they are used for repairing the stable or barn, or later for making bars on the doors. The inhabitants suffer the same fate. Each one plays his part as long as he can, then reluctantly withdraws into the ranks of the 'unuseables' and finally, attracting little attention, sinks into oblivion. The man who returns to us after years abroad finds nothing changed, except for a few old roofs that have been renewed and a few newer ones that have aged. The old men of his early days have vanished from the scene, but other old men are living in the same huts, bear the same names, keep an eye on the same dark-haired children and are scarcely distinguishable in face and bearing from those who have meanwhile died.

What our community needed was a more frequent supply of fresh life and blood from outside. The inhabitants, a rudely vigorous race, are mostly related, and a good three quarters of them share the same name, Camenzind. It fills the pages of the parish register, is carved on the tombstones, is picked out in paint or crudely carved on the houses and is also to be read on the carts, stable-buckets and lake boats. Over my father's own front door too, the following words were painted: 'Jost and Franziska Camenzind built this house', which did not refer to my father but to one of his ancestors, my great-grandfather, and when I too come to die even if childless, I can do so assured that another Camenzind will inhabit the old place provided it has a roof and is still standing.

Despite an apparent uniformity, there were among our number in the village good and bad, high-born and lowly, distinguished and ordinary people. And side by side with many intelligent inhabitants flourished a small, amusing minority of fools, excluding, of course, the village idiots. Here as everywhere else, existed a miniature world; and, since broad-mindedness and triviality, the cunning and the foolish were inextricably mixed and interbred, it was not unusual to discover overweening pride and shallow frivolity under the same roof, so that our lives provided ample scope both for the serious and comic side of human nature. Yet a permanent veil of unconscious or hidden uneasiness hung over them. Dependence on the powers of nature combined with the wretchedness of a life of unrelieved hard work had, in the course of the years, given our ageing breed a tendency to melancholy which, suited though it may have been to our rough, angular faces, failed to produce any fruit, or at least anything particularly agreeable. That was why we appreciated the presence of the sprinkling of fools who were, in all conscience, quiet and serious enough, but who provided a touch of colour and an outlet for laughter and mockery. Whenever an incident or escapade caused one of them to be gossiped about, a flash of merriment would pass over the wrinkled faces of the inhabitants of Nimikon, and the feeling of one's own superiority added piquancy to the joke. One tut-tutted all the more because one felt oneself to be immune to such weaknesses or aberrations. My father belonged to the majority, that is to those who stood half-way between the righteous and the sinners and were eager to enjoy any contribution from either party. Every mischief that was hatched filled him with pious uneasiness, and it was amusing to see him steering a hesitant course between respect for the instigator and the smug consciousness of his own guiltlessness.

Uncle Konrad belonged to the 'fools', though he was certainly no less intelligent than my own father or other heroes. Actually he was a sly fox, animated by a restless spirit of invention which the others might well have quietly envied. Yet, nothing went right for him. The fact that, instead of allowing himself to be shame-faced and ineffectually depressed about it, he was for ever starting up some new scheme, thereby showing a remarkable appreciation of the tragi-comic aspect of his own undertakings, could certainly be accounted a virtue in him; it was however ascribed to comic eccentricity and merely earned him a place among the unpaid jesters of the community. My father's relation with him alternated between scorn and admiration. Each of his brother-in-law's new schemes roused his intense curiosity and excitement which he vainly endeavoured to conceal behind cunningly ironic questions and insinuations. When my uncle felt convinced of his success and began to put on airs, my father allowed himself to be carried away, and, in a spirit of speculative brotherly affection, would associate himself with the genius until the inevitable catastrophe, which my uncle shrugged off while my father, furious, heaped insults and imprecations on his head and refused to favour him with a word or even a glance for months on end.

It was to Konrad that our village owed its first sight of a sailing-boat, and my father's skiff had to suffer in the process. The sail and rigging were skilfully made after calendar woodcuts by my uncle who could hardly be blamed for our skiff ultimately lacking the necessary beam to carry a sail. The preparations went on for weeks; my father was like a cat on hot bricks as a result of successive periods of suspense, hope and apprehension, and even among the village folk Konrad's scheme became the sole topic. That windy morning in late summer when the boat was to make its maiden voyage was unforgettable. Filled with forebodings of disaster, my father kept away, and, to my great annoyance, also refused to allow me to join the trip. The son of Füssli, the baker, was the only one permitted to accompany the expert sailor. But the whole village stood on our gravelled patch and in our garden to witness the fantastic sight. A squally east wind was blowing over the lake. To begin with, the baker's boy had to row until the breeze caught the sail, bellied it out, and the boat forged proudly ahead. Full of admiration, we watched it disappear round the nearest mountain spur and prepared to accord my clever uncle a victor's welcome on his return journey and to do penance for our earlier, disloyal doubts. But when, at night, the boat came home, she had lost her sail and the 'crew' were more dead than alive. Between fits of spluttering the baker's son said: 'You've all missed a grand treat; you nearly had a couple of funeral celebrations for next Sunday!' Father had to replace two boards in the boat, and from that day on no sail has ever disported itself on our lake's blue surface. For a long time afterwards whenever Konrad seemed in a hurry, they shouted 'Hoist your sails, Konrad!' Father bottled up his anger and for a long time he averted his gaze every time he encountered his wretched brother-in-law and spat to indicate his contempt. This situation continued until one day Konrad discussed with him his idea of a fire-proof oven; a scheme which brought permanent ridicule on the inventor's head and cost my father four *taler*. Woe to anyone who ventured to remind him of this four *taler* episode. Much later, when, once again, a financial crisis occured in the house my mother casually remarked that it would be wonderful if only they still had the money that had been so criminally wasted. My father turned purple in the face but controlled himself and only remarked 'I wish I had swilled it all away on a Sunday!'

The end of each winter was announced by the *Föhn*, accompanied by the hollow roar which the alpine dweller hears with trembling and horror and yet increasingly longs for when he is away from home. When the *Föhn* is on its way, its presence can be detected several hours beforehand by men and women, mountains, bird and beast. Its arrival, usually heralded by chilly gusts from the opposite quarter, is announced by a rich, deep roar. The blue-green lake-water is soon an inky black, and swift, white waves suddenly arise. The lake which only a moment before lay calm and silent, thunders against the shores like an angry sea. At the same time the whole landscape shrinks in terror. It is then possible to count the rocky spurs on mountain peaks which shortly before were brooding in the remote distance, and in villages which previously looked like brown flecks, one can distinguish the roofs, gables and windows of the houses. Everything appears to close in – mountains, meadows, houses – like a panic-stricken herd of cattle. Then starts a muffled roar; the ground shakes. Whipped-up waves are driven through wide stretches of air like smoke and the desperate battle between storm and mountain rings continually in your ears; especially in the night. Shortly after, news runs through the village of flooding rivers, stricken homes, wrecked boats, of fathers and brothers missing.

In childhood days, I was afraid of the *Föhn*; I even hated it. But with the dawn of my adolescent wildness, I grew to love this rebel, this perennially young, insolent fighter; the herald of Spring. It was glorious to see it embark on its mad career, full of life, exuberance and hope, raging, laughing, moaning, howling down the gulleys, whipping the snow from the mountains, bending the rough old pines in its strong hands, wresting great sighs from them. Later on my affection for it deepened, and then I welcomed in the *Föhn* the sweet, beautiful, luxuriant South from which joy, warmth and beauty continually gushed forth and finally burst among the mountains, only to bleed to death, exhausted, in the cold plains of the North. Nothing could be stranger or more precious than the gentle *Föhn* fever that overcomes the mountain-dwellers, especially their womenfolk, robbing them of their sleep, bewitching all their senses. It is the South hurling itself with all its heat and violence against the breast of the poorer, inflexible North, announcing the news to the snow-covered Alpine villages that primroses, narcissi and almond trees are once again in flower by the shores of the not too far distant purple lakes of Italy. When the *Föhn* has blown itself out and the grimy avalanches have swept by, the best of the season is at hand. On every side, the blossoming yellow meadows stretch up to the mountains; snowcapped peaks and glaciers stand pure and contented. The lake becomes blue and warm and reflects the sunlight and processions of clouds.

All these natural events can fill childhood and, if need be, a lifetime. For they proclaim loudly and uninterruptedly the message of God as it never came from the lips of man. Whoever has thus once heard it in childhood, hears it for the rest of his life, sweet, strong, fearful, and never escapes its spell. If one is a native of the mountains, one can study philosophy or natural history for years and do away with the God of old, and yet as one feels the *Föhn* approach once more or hears an avalanche break through the thicket, your heart throbs in your breast and your thoughts turn to God and to death.

My father's hut bordered on a tiny, fenced garden where there grew bitter lettuces, carrots and cabbages. In addition, my mother had prepared a touchingly small flower-bed in which a couple of china roses, a dahlia and a handful of mignonette languished hopelessly and miserably. Next to our garden was a still smaller gravelled patch which stretched as far as the lake. There stood two damaged barrels, some boards and fencestakes, and moored in the water below was our punt, which in those days was repaired and caulked every few years. The days on which these operations were carried out are still firmly fixed in my memory. They were warm, early summer afternoons; over the garden the brimstones fluttered in the sunlight, the lake was as smooth as oil, blue and motionless, softly iridescent, the mountain tops were thinly veiled in mist and the little gravelled patch smelt strongly of tar and paint. Even afterwards, the boat smelt strongly of tar throughout the summer. Many years later, whenever by the sea I came upon this peculiar smell, of tar and water, I would at once see our little gravelled landing-place and my father, in his shirt-sleeves, plying his paint-brush, and the blue smoke from his pipe curling up in the still summer air, and the vivid yellow butterflies essaying their shy, unsteady flights. On such days, my father revealed himself in an unusually congenial frame of mind, whistled trills which he could do excellently, and would even indulge in a short burst of yodelling, half-aloud to himself. Meantime, mother would be cooking something good for the evening meal, and, as it seems to me, with the secret hope that her husband would refrain from visiting the inn that evening. But he went all the same.

I cannot claim that my parents had a particularly good or bad influence on the development of my youthful character. Mother always had her hands full with work, and there was certainly nothing in the world which had bothered my father less than his children's upbringing. He had enough to do tending his handful of miserable fruit-trees, cultivating his small potato field and seeing to his hay crop. Sometimes however, before he went out in the evening, he took me by the hand and led me in silence to the loft over the stable. There, a strange rite of chastisement and atonement took place. I received a good thrashing without either my father or myself quite knowing exactly the reason. They were silent sacrifices on the altar of Nemesis and were offered as due tribute to a secret power, unaccompanied by any scolding on his part or complaints on mine. When, in later years, I heard people talk about 'Blind Fate', these mysterious scenes would come back to me, and appeared to me as the concrete manifestation of that conception. Unconsciously, my good father was following the simple teaching of life when it inflicts a thunderstorm on us, leaving us to reflect by what misdeeds we have provoked the Powers above.

Unfortunately this reflection seldom occurred to me. For the most part, I accepted each instalment of punishment, resigned or even resentful, without the self-examination that seemed expected of me, only too relieved on such evenings that I had once more paid my toll and could enjoy a few week's respite from punishment. I adopted a far more independent attitude to my father's efforts to persuade me to work. Mysterious, prodigal nature had seen fit to combine

two contradictory qualities in me – unusual physical strength
with a strong disinclination to work. My father went to considerable trouble to make a useful son and helpmate of me,
but I resorted to every possible subterfuge to avoid the tasks
imposed on me, and, while still a schoolboy, I regarded no
hero of antiquity with more sympathy than Hercules, since
he carried out his tiresome and famous labours under com-
pulsion. Meanwhile, my greatest joy was to idle among the
rocks and meadows or by the water. Mountains, lake, storm
and sun were my familiars; they talked to me and brought
me up; for long they had been dearer and closer to me than
any human being or human fate. What I loved however above
all else, even more than the glistening waters, the melancholy
pine-trees and sun-drenched rocks, were the clouds.

Find me a man in the whole wide world who knows and
loves the clouds more than I! Show me anything that is more
beautiful! They represent the spirit of play, the wrath of
heaven and the power of death; they are a comfort to the eye,
a blessing and a gift of God, as tender, yielding and gentle
as the souls of new-born children. They are as handsome,
rich and prodigal as Good Angels; as sombre, inescapable and
merciless as messengers of death. They sweep by in silvery
wisps, sail along, white, jocund masses lined with gold; they
hang poised, tinged with yellow, red and blue. Darkly and
slowly they glide past like murderers; chase helter-skelter like
mad horsemen, linger sad and dreamily on the pale heights
like melancholy hermits. They assume the shapes of the
blessed isles and of guardian angels, of threatening hands,
fluttering sails, cranes in flight. They journey between God's
heaven and our poor earth, glorious images of all man's
yearning, and belonging to both – dreams of the earth in
which its blemished soul cleaves to the pure heaven above.
They are the eternal symbol of all voyaging, all questing, all
yearning for home. Like they who are suspended, faint-
hearted yet defiant and nostalgic between heaven and earth,
the souls of human beings sharing the same emotions are
suspended between time and eternity.

O lovely, restless floating clouds! I was an ignorant child but I loved and contemplated them, little knowing that I too should go through life like a cloud, wandering, everywhere a stranger, floating between time and eternity. Ever since childhood days they have been my dear friends and sisters. I cannot even cross the road without exchanging a greeting with them while we linger a moment and gaze at each other. Nor did I ever forget what I learned at that time; their features, shapes, colours, games and frolics; their strange, fantastic tales. Most of all I remember the Snow Princess. Her stage is on the lower mountains in early winter, among the warm under-currents of air. The Snow Princess appears with a small retinue, descending from the great heights, and seeks a resting-place for herself in distant mountain-hollows or upon a broad summit. Envious, the false North wind sees the innocent maiden lie down to rest, in secret lust leaps up the mountain and suddenly falls upon her in rage and fury, hurls torn shreds of black cloud in the beautiful Princess's direction, shouts at her and tries to drive her away. For a while the Princess is ill at ease, waits patiently and often climbs back to her heights, shaking her head in gentle scorn. Often too, however, she gathers her frightened maids-in-waiting around her, unveils her dazzlingly regal countenance and waves the evil spirit boldly back. He hesitates, howls and flees away. And she lies down quietly, shrouds her throne in white mist, and when the mist has withdrawn, valleys and mountain tops lie bright and gleaming in their covering of pure, soft new snow.

This story had such an element of nobility, soulfulness and triumphant beauty that my heart was stirred and entranced as by a happy secret.

The time was at hand when I should draw closer to the clouds, move among them and would be vouchsafed a view of many of their host from above. I was ten years old when I climbed my first mountain, the Sennalpstock, at the foot of which lies our small village of Nimikon. Then it was that I beheld for the first time the terrors and the attractions of the mountains. Deeply cleft gulleys, filled with ice and half-melted snow, smooth, green glasslike glaciers, awe-inspiring moraine, and, above it all like a bell, high and dome-like, the sky. When you have lived for ten years, hemmed in between mountain and lake and closely bounded by neighbouring heights, you do not easily forget your first day with a vast heaven extending above and a limitless horizon ahead. Even during the ascent, I was amazed to find crags and cliffs, familiar to me from below, so overpoweringly huge. And now, quite overcome by the moment, with a feeling of awe and jubilation, I suddenly saw this vast space bearing down on me. So the world was as big as that! Our whole village, lying lost in the depths below, was only one small, light-coloured speck. Peaks which viewed from our valley I had thought of as close together, lay many hours' march apart. Then I began to realize that, so far, I had had a very limited glimpse of the world, not a real view at all, and that beyond, the mountains could stand or fall, great events take place without any whisper of them ever reaching our remote Alpine village. At the same time, however, something within me quivered like a compass-needle in involuntary but irresistible yearning for those far-off places. It was only when I saw what infinite stretches they covered that I appreciated the beauty and the melancholy of the clouds.

Both the grown-ups who accompanied me praised my climbing, rested awhile on the ice-cold summit and laughed at my unbounded enthusiasm. But when I recovered from my great initial astonishment, I bellowed in the clear air like a bull, out of sheer joy and excitement. It was my first, in-articulate hymn to beauty. I expected a resounding echo, but my voice died away unanswered among the peaceful heights like a faint bird-cry. I felt ashamed and kept silent.

That day was a landmark in my life. For now, one event followed another. In the first place, the men often took me with them on mountain ascents, even difficult ones, and it was with a strange feeling of uneasy ecstasy that I penetrated the great secrets of their summits.

Then I was made goatherd. On one of the slopes where I used to take my beasts was a corner sheltered from the wind; it was starred with cobalt-blue gentians and bright-red saxifrage. It was my favourite haunt. From there the village was not visible, and away over the rocks only a narrow gleaming strip of the lake-water could be seen; but the flowers glowed in their fresh colours, the blue sky hung like a canopy over the rugged snow-covered peaks, and the thin tinkle of the goat-bells could be heard against the continual murmur of a nearby waterfall. There I lay in the warmth, gazing full of wonder at the small white clouds and yodelled half aloud to myself until the goats exploited my laziness and got up to all kinds of mischief. Even in the first weeks my idyllic interlude suffered a rude interruption when I fell down a gully with a stray goat. The goat died and I injured my head; I was also unmercifully beaten, ran away from my parents, and brought back home amid curses and lamentations.

These adventures might well have been my first and last. In that case this book would have remained unwritten and I should have been spared many trials and much foolishness. I would probably have married one of my cousins and eventually been frozen to death on the edge of a glacier. There could be worse prospects. But things happened otherwise, and it is pointless to compare what did not occur with what did.

My father used to do some small job from time to time in the Welsdörf monastery. On one occasion he became ill and told me to notify the monastery that he would be unable to come. Instead, I borrowed pen and paper from a neighbour and wrote a courteous letter to the Friars which I gave to the woman who carried messages, and wandered into the mountains alone.

One day, the following week, I came home and there was a priest waiting for the person who had penned such a good letter. I felt somewhat apprehensive, but he praised me and tried to persuade my father to let him teach me. Uncle Konrad, who had now come back into favour, was asked for his opinion. Naturally he was eager for me to study and eventually become a scholar and a gentleman. My father let himself be persuaded, and my future now took its place alongside my uncle's other dangerous and hair-brained schemes, such as the fireproof oven and the sailing-boat.

A formidable programme of instruction which included Latin, divinity, botany and geography was immediately inaugurated. I found all this very entertaining but I failed to realize that this extraneous knowledge might cost me my home, and years of happiness. Nor was Latin solely to blame. My father would have made a landworker of me even had I known the whole *Viri Illustres* by heart. But the shrewd priest had probed deep into my temperament, the seat of invincible idleness, my centre of gravity and besetting sin. I dodged work whenever possible and made off into the mountains or the lake or lay hidden on the hillside; read, dreamed and idled. Realizing this, my father finally let me go.

It seems an appropriate moment to say a brief word about my parents. My mother had been handsome in her time but now her straight, well-built frame and attractive, dark eyes were all that remained of her beauty. She was tall, extremely strong, hard-working and quiet. Although she was certainly as clever as my father and physically superior, she did not rule the house, but left him to dictate. He was of average build, but with thin, almost frail limbs, a sly, obstinate head and a face of fair complexion, covered with tiny, unusually mobile wrinkles. He also had a low, vertical furrow on his brow which darkened and gave him a morose, ailing expression whenever he frowned. He looked as if he were striving to remember some matter of grave import without any hope of recalling it. One might have detected his inherent melancholy, but it passed unnoticed, for almost all the inhabitants of our locality are victims of continuous, gentle melancholy no doubt encouraged by the long winters and their attendant dangers, the painful struggle for life and isolation from the world outside.

I have inherited important elements of my temperament

from both parents. From my mother: a modest worldly wisdom; a trust in God; a calm, taciturn disposition. From my father, on the other hand: a dread of firm resolutions; an inability to keep money and the habit of consciously drinking more than was good for me. But the latter defect had not revealed itself in those tender years. Outwardly, I have my father's eyes and mouth, and my mother's slow, heavy gait; her build and strength. From my father and our people in general I inherited a natural peasant cunning, but also their melancholy and their tendency to unaccountable fits of depression. Since for years it was my destiny to intermingle with foreigners, far from my native village, I would have been better equipped with more gaiety, more lightheartedness.

With these provisions, and a new set of clothes, I set forth on my journey into life. My parental gifts have stood me well, for I went out into the world, and have stood on my own feet ever since. Yet something must have been lacking which even knowledge and experience has not righted. Even today I can still vanquish a mountain, walk ten hours at a stretch, row a boat and, if necessary, I could kill a man with my bare hands, but the art of living still eludes me. My early, single-minded contact with the earth, its flora and fauna, has allowed few social graces to blossom in me, and to this day my dreams are a remarkable proof of my unfortunate tendency towards a purely animal existence. I frequently dream that I am a creature lying on the shore, usually a seal, and I am conscious of such an intense feeling of well-being that on waking, I return to human dignity, not with pride or rejoicing, but only with regret.

I was brought up in the usual way with free board and tuition at a Grammar School, and I was intended to be a classic. Heaven knows why, for no course of study is more tedious and none lay further from my grasp.

My schoolboy years passed in a flash. Between fights and lessons, I spent hours of home-sickness, of bold dreams for the future; hours of devoted worship of knowledge. But here also my innate laziness intervened, bringing me all kinds of punishment, and then gradually some new enthusiasm would fill me.

'Peter Camenzind,' said my Greek teacher, 'you are an obstinate fellow, an individualist; you'll break your head against a brick wall yet.' I surveyed the corpulent, bespectacled teacher, listened to his speech and found him amusing.

'Peter Camenzind,' remarked the mathematics master, 'you have a genius for idling and my only regret is that nought is the lowest mark, for I assess your exercise today at minus two and a half!' I stared at him, with a certain sympathy because he was cross-eyed, and so extremely boring.

'Peter Camenzind,' said the history teacher on one occasion, 'you are a bad scholar, but you will become a good historian, all the same. You are lazy, but you know the difference between great and trivial things.'

But even that quality did not strike me as particularly important. Still, I regarded the teachers with a certain respect, for I thought they had a monopoly of knowledge, and of knowledge I had a vague, indefinable awe. And although the teachers all agreed about my laziness I made some progress and was more than halfway up the class. I realized that school and school knowledge consisted of an inadequate patchwork, but I was biding my time. I divined the truly intellectual, pure, unambiguous, certain knowledge of truth behind those tentative preparations and fumblings. One day, in those kingdoms of knowledge I would discover what the sombre confusion of history, the battles between nations and the frightening question within each human soul meant. But I was conscious of a still stronger and more powerful yearning – I longed for a friend.

There was a serious, brown-haired boy, two years older than I, called Kaspar Hauri. He had a quiet confident air, bore his head in a manly, resolute and grave manner, and spoke little to his comrades. For months I looked up to him with great veneration, followed him about in the street, and longed to win his approval. I was jealous of every dull citizen whom he greeted, of every house I saw him enter and leave. But I was two classes below him, and he, no doubt, already felt superior to his own. No word was exchanged between us. Instead, and without any encouragement, a puny, sickly boy attached himself to me. He was younger than I, timid and not very bright, but he had beautiful eyes with a touch of suffering in them. Because he was weakly and slightly mis-shapen, he was subjected to a great deal of bullying in his class, and he looked to me for protection because I was strong and respected. Very soon he became too ill to attend school. I did not miss him, and quickly forgot him.

Then there was a boisterous fair-haired boy in our class who was extremely versatile – musician, mimic, and clown. I won his friendship though not without effort, and my cheerful little contemporary always adopted a slightly superior attitude towards me. All the same, I now had a friend. I sought him out in his small study, read a few books with him, did his Greek exercises, and in return I enlisted his help for my mathematics. We also went on many walks together and must indeed have looked an ill assorted couple. He did all the talk-ing, gay, witty and completely at ease; and I listened and laughed, happy to have such a light-hearted companion.

One afternoon I unexpectedly came upon him just when the little hypocrite was doing one of his favourite acts to some friends in the school corridor. He had been impersonating one of the masters and now he was calling out. 'Guess who this is!' and at the same time began to read a few lines of Homer. He was giving a faithful imitation of me, my awkward bearing, my nervous reading, my rough country accent and of my per-petual habit when concentrating, of blinking and shutting my left eye. It looked very funny and the performance was quite ruthless. When he had shut the book and collected his well-deserved applause, I strode up behind him and took my revenge. Words failed me, but I summoned all my indigna-tion, shame and fury into one purposeful and terrific cuff on his ear. Immediately afterwards the lesson began, and the master noticed the sound of whimpering and the swollen red cheeks of my erstwhile friend who was also his favourite pupil.

'Who has done that to you?'

'Camenzind.'

'Camenzind, come out! Is it true?'

'Yes, sir.'

'Why did you hit him?'

No reply.

'Did you have any reason for doing it?'

'No, sir.'

So I was severely punished, and I wallowed in the bliss of innocent martyrdom. But as I was neither stoic nor saint but a schoolboy, after my chastisement I stuck my tongue out at my enemy, to its full length. Horrified the master let fly at me.

'Aren't you ashamed of yourself? What is the meaning of this?'

'It means that he is a dirty rat and I despise him. And he is a coward too.'

So my friendship with the mimic came to an end. He had no successor, and I had to spend the years of my adolescence without a friend. But although my views on life and the human race have since changed to some extent, I never recall that box on the ear without feelings of profound satisfaction. I trust that my fair-haired friend has not forgotten it either.

At seventeen, I fell in love with a solicitor's daughter. She was good-looking, and I am proud of the fact that all through my life I have only fallen in love with extremely beautiful women. What I suffered because of her and other women, I will relate another time. Her name was Rösi Girtanner and to this day she is worthy of the love of better men than me.

At that time the fresh vigour of youth still coursed through my limbs. I was being for ever involved in scraps with my school-mates. I preened myself on being the best wrestler, ball hitter, runner and oarsman, in spite of which I was always melancholy. It had little to do with my love affair. It was merely the agreeable melancholy of early Spring which

22

affected me more than the others, so that I derived pleasure from melancholy fancies, thoughts of death and pessimistic reflections. Naturally there was also a friend there to give me Heine's lyrics to read in a cheap edition! Nor was it a question merely of reading – I poured out my overflowing heart into the empty verses, suffered with the poet, composed verses of my own parallel to his and was intoxicated with poetry that probably suited me about as well as a frill round a pig's neck. Up till then I had no idea of 'fine literature'. Next came Lenau, Schiller, then Goethe and Shakespeare and suddenly the pale phantom Literature had become elevated to a great godhead.

With a delicious shudder I felt the fragrant coolness stream from these books towards me, I breathed a rarefied atmosphere of a life which though real enough did not seem of this world. It was this life that sent its waves pounding against my stricken heart and I was eager to share its fate. I used to read in a corner of the attic. There, where the only sounds that reached me were the chimes from the neighbouring tower and the dry flapping of the wings of the nesting storks, the characters of Goethe and Shakespeare made their exits and their entrances. The godlike and comic side of all humanity rose before me – the enigma of our divided, unruly heart, the reality of the world's history and the mighty wonder of the spirit that illuminates our brief span of life, and, through the power of discernment, raises our petty existence to the realm of the necessary and eternal. Whenever I put my head out of the narrow window, I saw the sun shine on roofs and narrow streets, and heard amazed, the noises of work and everyday activity rise up mingling together; I felt the loneliness and secrecy of my attic, inhabited with the great souls of the past, encompass me like some strangely beautiful fairy tale. And gradually as I read more and was more strangely moved by my view down onto the roof-tops, streets and everyday life below, the feeling, mixed with doubts and hesitations, came over me that I too perhaps was a visionary, and the world that lay before me was waiting for me to collect some portion of its treasure, to lift the veil from the accidental and common-place, and, through my creative power of poetry, save from destruction and immortalize whatever I might discover.

Somewhat shamefacedly I began to compose a little poetry and gradually several notebooks were filled with verses, sketches and short stories. They have perished and were probably of little worth, but they provided me with many thrills and much secret ecstacy. Only by a slow process did my critical powers and powers of self-examination keep pace with these attempts, and only in my last year at school did I suffer the inevitable, first great disappointment. I had already begun to throw away my *juvenalia* and to examine my writings with misgivings when I chanced upon some volumes of the works of Gottfried Keller. I immediately read these two or three times in succession. Then I saw in a sudden revelation how far removed from true, austere, genuine art my immature vapourings had been, burned my verses and short stories, and with feelings of pain and depression looked sadly and soberly into the world.

Chapter Two

Where love is concerned, I must confess to having remained a child all my life. For love for women has always been for me a purifying act of devotion - a tall flame mounting upward from my melancholy, praying hands stretched towards the blue heavens. Prompted by my love for my mother and vague feelings within, I have always honoured the female sex as a strange and mysterious race superior to the male by virtue of its inherent beauty and singleness of being and one to be regarded as divine because, like the stars and blue mountain peaks, it is remote from us and seems nearer to heaven. And since life has not spared me many harsh experiences, I have suffered as much bitterness as sweetness from the love of women, and although they have never left their lofty pedestal, my own solemn role of acolyte was all too easily transformed into the tragicomic one of a despised buffoon.

I met Rösi Girtanner almost every day on my way home to dinner. She was a girl of seventeen, strongly built yet supple. Her narrow face with its dark, flawless complexion radiated the same quiet, spiritual beauty still possessed by her mother and which her grandmother and great-grandmother had possessed before her. This distinguished old family had produced a fine long line of women, each of a quiet, noble and unblemished beauty. The *Portrait of a Young Girl of the Fugger family*, painted by an Unknown Master in the sixteenth century still exists and I consider it one of the best pictures I have ever seen. All the Girtanner women resembled it and Rösi was no exception.

Naturally I was unaware of all this at the time. I merely saw her moving around in her gay, quiet dignity and was conscious of the distinction of her unaffected character. I would sit reflecting in the evening half-light until I succeeded in conjuring up her presence clearly before me. A delicious shudder would run through my boyish heart. Soon however, these blissful moments were overcast and caused me bitter sorrow. I suddenly realized how remote she was from me: she neither knew me nor inquired after me: my lovely vision was merely an intrusion in her blessed existence. And even when I felt acutely and distressingly aware of this I still saw her image before me so real and alive that a dark warm tide flooded my heart and made every nerve in my body ache.

In the daytime these waves would suddenly overwhelm me in the middle of class or during a tussle with some other boy. I would close my eyes, let my hands fall and feel myself sliding down into a warm abyss until my teacher's voice or a classmate's fist jerked me back to rude reality. Then I would dash off outside and stare into the world beyond with a sensation of wonderful dreaminess. I would suddenly see how lovely, how full of colour everything was: how sight and breath flowed through every living thing, how transparently green the river was, how red the roofs, how blue the mountains were. But this ubiquitous beauty did not distract me: I savoured it quietly and sadly. The more beautiful everything was, the stranger it seemed to me who stood outside and had no part in it. So my benumbed thoughts found their way back to Rösi, and how, if I were to die at that moment she would neither know nor inquire about it, nor even feel distressed. Yet to win her attention was not what mattered most to me. I would gladly have performed some wonderful deed or produced some offering for her without her knowing who her benefactor was. In fact I accomplished many feats for her. It was at the time of a short holiday break and I was sent home. There I subjected myself every day to every kind of test, all to Rösi's honour and glory. I climbed a difficult peak from the steepest side, I made fantastic excursions in the boat on the lake, covering incredible distances in short spaces of time. As I returned from one of these journeys, dried up and hungry, it occurred to me to go without food and drink until evening. All for Rösi Girtanner's sake. I bore her name and glory to distant summits and gulleys where no human foot had trodden. At the same time my youth, too cramped by the classroom, found a joyful outlet in the process. My shoulders broadened out, my face and neck became weathered and my muscles swelled and expanded.

On the last day but one of the holidays I took my sweetheart a posy of flowers, won at great peril. I knew of course that Edelweiss grew on narrow earth-filled crevices on several tempting slopes, but that sickly, silvery flower without scent or colour had always seemed to me lifeless and unattractive. On the other hand I knew of a few isolated Alpine roses, secluded in the cleft of a steep precipice. They had blossomed late, and to reach them presented a challenge. But reach them I must. And since nothing is impossible to youth and love, I finally reached my goal with lacerated hands and cramp in my legs. To shout for joy in the alarming position in which I found myself was a physical impossibility but my heart yodelled within me as I carefully severed the tough stalks and held my prey in my hands. I now had to accomplish the climb in reverse, holding the flowers between my teeth and heaven knows how, after this foolhardy exploit, I ever reached the foot of the cliff-wall intact. The Alpine roses on the whole mountain range had withered long ago, but in my hands I held the last sprays of the season, budding and blooming.

Next day I carried them cupped in my hands throughout the five hour journey. At the start, my heart beat with excitement to reach my lovely Rösi's town; the further I left the high mountain behind however, the stronger I felt my innate love for it tugging at me. I remember that railway journey so clearly. The Sennalpstock had long since passed out of sight; now the rugged foothills disappeared one after the other and each one sank away from my heart leaving me with a feeling of regret. Now all the familiar peaks had vanished and a broad, lower, bright-green landscape thrust itself into view. It was a sight that had failed to affect me on my first journey

But this time I was overcome by uneasiness, fear and melancholy, as if I had been condemned to travel further and further into level plains and lose irretrievably my hills and the freedom of my native place. At the same time I had a picture of Rösi's narrow face in front of me, looking so refined, strange and unconcerned about me that my breath froze with bitterness and anguish. Those gay, spotless villages with their slender steeples and white gables slipped by one after another as I gazed from the carriage window. Passengers got in and out, chatted, haled one another, laughed, smoked and joked - cheerful lowlanders, everyone of them, smart bland, unaffected folk - and I, a stolid youth from the mountains, sat among them, silent and morose, out of my element. I felt that I had been torn away from my hills for ever without any hope of becoming as cheerful, adept, bland and self-assured as they. Their kind would always be able to make fun of me; the Girtanner girl would marry one of them some day; one of them would always be in my path and a pace ahead.

Such were the thoughts that I took with me to the town. There, after a preliminary exchange of greetings I went up to the loft, opened my trunk and extracted a sheet of note-paper. It wasn't of very good quality and by the time I had wrapped my Alpine roses in it and tied it round with a piece of string I had brought from home, the parcel did not much resemble a love-token. I solemnly took it down into the street where the lawyer, Herr Girtanner lived and at the first favourable opportunity I stepped through the open door, looked about me in the hall, dim in the dusk, and deposited my clumsy parcel on the broad impressive staircase. No one saw me and I never discovered whether Rösi had noticed my greeting. But the fact remained that I had climbed down precipices and risked my life to lay a spray of Alpine roses on the staircase of her home, and there was something bitter-sweet, something poetic about the enterprise that produced a warm glow inside me. Even to this day I can recapture the feeling. Only in my more despairing moods does it sometimes seem to me that the Rösi adventure was a piece of quixotry and no different from all my subsequent love-affairs.

So this first love episode of mine never came to a conclusion; instead, it echoed enigmatically all through my youthful years and accompanied my later love-affairs like a quiet elder sister. Nor have I ever succeeded in imagining anyone nobler, purer, lovelier than that young, calm-eyed patrician's daughter. When, many years later, I saw that strangely attractive anonymous portrait of the Fugger daughter in a historical exhibition in Munich, I seemed to see my sad, enchanted youth before me gazing forlornly at me from the depths of its unfathomable eyes.

Meantime slowly and solemnly I cast off my slough and gradually became a full-blooded youth. The photograph taken of me at that time shows a bony, overgrown peasant lad in shabby school clothes with rather dull eyes and ungainly limbs. Only the head reveals a certain doggedness and precocity. With a kind of astonishment I watched myself leave my boyhood ways behind, and looked ahead to my student days with sombre anticipation. I was to study at Zurich, and, if I did particularly well, my patrons had proposed sending me on a cultural tour. This conjured up in my mind a beautiful, classical picture. I saw a solemn, friendly grove adorned with the busts of Homer and Plato, and myself sitting there head bowed over learned tomes, surrounding me was a wide, clear view over town, lake and mountains with enticing prospects beyond. I had become more dispassionate but more energetic and I looked forward to my future good fortune with the firm conviction that I should prove worthy of it.

In my last year at school I was absorbed in the study of Italian and had had my first introduction to the old story-writers whom I had selected as my special subject for the first semester at the university. Then the day came for me to say goodbye to my teachers and the housemaster and to pack and fasten my small trunk and, taking my leave with cheerful melancholy, I hung about outside Rösi's house.

The holiday period which now followed gave me a bitter foretaste of life and soon put an end to my idealistic dreams. My first shock was to find my mother ill. She lay in bed, scarcely speaking and paid little heed to my arrival. I was not prone to self-pity, nevertheless I was upset that my joy and youthful pride evoked no response in her. Then my father explained that he certainly had no objection to my studying but that he was unable to provide the money for it. If the small scholarship did not suffice I would have to set about earning the balance myself. By the time he was my age he had long been earning his living. And so on . . .

I was unable to indulge in much walking, rowing and climbing because I had to work either at home or in the fields, and on free afternoons I had little inclination for anything, even reading. I was wearied and indignant as I became aware how much the common daily task exacted its dues and absorbed all that was left of my high spirits and energy. And once my father had relieved himself of my money problems as abrupt and harsh as he may have been with me, he was not unsympathetic. But that was no consolation. I was disturbed and pained by the fact that my school education and books merely earned his silent, half-contemptuous respect. And then my thoughts were often centred round Rösi and once again I felt wretchedly and resentfully aware of my peasant inability ever to become a respectable and energetic adult in the outside world. Indeed, for days on end I wondered whether it would be better to forget my Latin and my hopes and to face the hard and grim battle for a livelihood in my native place. Irritated and anxious, I strolled about finding neither comfort nor peace by the bedside of my sick mother. The picture of that dream-grove with the bust of Homer became a mockery, so I destroyed it and heaped it with all the emnity and vituperation of my tortured being. The weeks became intolerably drawn-out, and it seemed as if I was destined to waste all my youth in this hopeless period of anger and frustration.

If I had been amazed and angry to see life destroy my

blissful dreams with such speed and thoroughness, I had now reached the stage of surprise at the power and rapidity with which one could gain mastery over existing torments. Life had revealed its grey workaday aspect and now it suddenly opened its eternal depths to my perplexed gaze and laid the burden of a sober and impressive experience on my youthful years.

Early in bed one hot summer morning, I felt thirsty and got up to go into the kitchen where there was always a tub of fresh water. To reach it I had to pass through my parents' bedroom where strange moans from my mother pulled me up abruptly. I approached her bed, but she neither saw me nor said anything. She merely continued her dry, frightened moans: her eyelids fluttered and her cheeks showed a bluish pallor. Though anxious, I was not particularly frightened. Then I noticed her hands lying motionless on the counterpane like a brother and sister asleep. They told me that my mother was dying, for they already looked strangely detached and deathly weary, unlike those of any living person. I forgot my thirst, knelt beside her bed, laid my hand on her brow and tried to meet her eyes. When at last our eyes met, hers were steadfast and untroubled but near extinction. It did not enter my mind to wake my father who was sleeping heavily close by. I knelt there for two hours and witnessed my mother suffer death. She did so with characteristically calm solemnity leaving me a noble example.

The little room was quiet. Slowly it filled with the brightness of the oncoming day; house and village lay asleep and I had the leisure to accompany in my mind the soul of a dying person, over house, village, lake and snow-covered peaks to the cool freedom of a pure, early morning sky. I felt little grief, for the great riddle of death and the gentle shudder that accompanied the end of a human life had filled me with awe and amazement. The uncomplaining courage of the departing spirit had been so dignified that a clear, refreshing ray of light from her simple glory seemed to penetrate my own soul. The fact that my father had been sleeping close by, that no priest had been present and that the homing soul had had neither sacrament nor prayers to accompany her on her last journey left me unmoved. All I felt was an awe-inspiring breath of eternity flooding through the dawn-lit room and mingling with my being. At the last moment when her eyes were already closed, I planted a kiss on my mother's cold, shrivelled lips for the first time in my life. Then with a sudden horror I felt the strange chill of this contact run through me and I sat on the edge of the bed while one large tear after another coursed down my checks and over my chin and hands.

Shortly after, my father woke up, noticed me sitting there and in a voice thick with sleep asked me what was the matter. I tried to reply but was unable to utter a word. I went out dazed, and found my way to my own room where, mechanically, I dressed. Soon my father appeared.

'Mother is dead,' he said. 'Did you know?' I nodded.

'Then why did you let me go on sleeping? And there wasn't even a priest with her! May you be . . .' He uttered a portentous curse.

I felt a great pain in my head as if a vein had burst. Then I gripped both his hands - in physical strength, he was a child compared to me - and stared into his face. I could not say anything, but he calmed down, seemed dazed, and when we went together to where my mother lay, the presence of death overwhelmed him too and brought a strange, solemn expression to his face. Then he bent over the body and began to sob softly like a child with feeble, almost birdlike cries. I left him and took the news to the neighbours. They listened to me, asking no questions, but holding out their hands they offered our bereaved household any help they could give. One of them ran down the road to the monastery to fetch a priest, and when I returned home, a neighbour was already in our cattle-stall, seeing to the cow.

The priest and almost every woman in the village came, and everything went off punctually and smoothly as if of its own accord. Even the coffin materialized without our intervention and for the first time I could see clearly the advantages of being among one's own people and belonging to a small, self-sufficient community in times of crisis. Perhaps the next day I ought to have reflected more deeply on the subject.

When prayers had been said over the coffin and it had been lowered into the grave, and the wonderful *cortège* of melancholy, old-fashioned top-hats, including my father's bristly beaver, had found their way back into their boxes and wardrobes, my father suddenly broke down. He began to indulge in self-pity and expatiated on his misery in strange, largely biblical phraseology, complaining that now his wife was buried he would have to see his son desert him for foreign countries. There was no end to it. I listened, horrified, and was almost on the point of promising to stay. At that moment – I had already framed my answer – I was overcome by a strange feeling. Suddenly everything that I had been thinking about and longing for from my earliest days flashed before me – telescoped as it were before my inner-eye which was for the first time opened. I saw noble tasks ahead of me involving the reading and writing of books. I heard the *Föhn* sweep by, caught glimpses of distant lakes and shores, shining in all the brilliance of the south. I saw people with clever intellectual faces and handsome, distinguished women go past. I saw country roads and mountain passes leading over the Alps and trains thundering across the landscape. It was simultaneous vision, yet each item was well-defined and separate, and behind all the boundless distance stretched a clear horizon interrupted by the scudding clouds. Scholarship, creation, travel, observation – life in all its richness and fulness shone in a fugitive, silver gleam before my eyes. And, once again as in my boyhood, something within me responded with an ecstatic shudder to the mighty challenge of the world's great spaces.

I fell silent and let my father talk on, content to shake my head and to wait until his emotion had spent itself. This was not until evening. I then explained to him my firm resolve to study and seek my future home in the realms of the intellect. At the same time I explained that I did not look to him for financial support. He stopped bullying me but looked depressed and shook his head. For even he realized that I was

3

now becoming independent and would soon be a complete stranger to his life. As I was setting down what I remembered of that episode, I seemed to see my father again that evening as he sat in a chair by the window. The solid, shrewd peasant head on the lean neck is motionless, his short hair is greying, and the harsh rugged features betray the fight his physical toughness is pitting against life's trials and the first onslaughts of old age.

There still remains one minor but not wholly insignificant event concerning my father which I must mention. One evening of the week before my departure he put on his cap and gripped the door-handle. 'Where are you going?' I asked. 'Mind your own business,' he replied. 'You would tell me if it wasn't something to be ashamed of,' I said. Then he laughed. 'You can join me if you like. You're no longer a child.' So I accompanied him to the local inn. A few peasants were sitting in front of a jug of *Hallauer* wine, a couple of foreign carriers were drinking absinth, some youths were noisily playing a game called 'Jass'. I was accustomed to drinking the occasional glass of wine but this was the first time I had called at the inn without a special reason. I knew from hearsay that my father could consume a good deal of alcohol. In fact he drank a lot, and good stuff too, which accounted for the perpetually poor state of things in the house, even though he could not be accused of serious neglect. I noticed that host and guests showed him marked respect. He ordered a litre of Vaud wine, bade me pour out and demonstrated how to set about it. You must pour it at a low angle, lengthen the jet and finally bring down the bottle as near to the glass as possible. At that point he began to expound on the various wines he knew and was accustomed to enjoy on his rare visits to the town or trips into French Switzerland. He spoke in portentous tones of the dark red *Veltliner*, and distinguished between three different kinds. From that, he proceeded talking in a soft, urgent voice about certain Vaud wines. Finally, in an almost confidential whisper and with the expression of a teller of fairy tales, he spoke about the wines of *Neuchâtel*. There were certain vintages of these in which the foam formed a star-shape when it was poured into the glass. And he drew a star on the table with his wetted fore-finger. Then he expatiated ponderously on character and fla-vour of champagne which, incidentally, he had never drunk and was under the illusion that one bottle could lay out a couple of people.

Silently and meditatively he lit his pipe and while so doing noticed that I hadn't anything to smoke and gave me ten centimes to buy some cigars. We then sat opposite each other, puffing smoke into each other's faces and slowly gulped down our first litre. The golden, piquant Vaud wine tasted excellent. Gradually the peasants at the next table started to join in the conversation and finally, and one by one with much depre-catory throat-clearing, they sat down next to us. Soon the interest centred on me and it became evident that my prowess as a climber had not been forgotten. All manner of hazardous climbs and mad descents veiled in legendary mist were re-counted, disputed and defended. Meantime we had almost finished the second litre and my eyes were terribly bloodshot. Quite out of character, I began to boast and recounted my audacious ascent to the upper Sennalpstock wall where I had plucked the Alpine roses for Rösi Girtanner. They refused to believe me; I protested and they laughed. I lost my temper and challenged anyone who didn't believe me to a wrestling match and added that if necessary I would take them all on. At that point a bent old peasant walked over to the counter, fetched a huge earthenware jug and laid it lengthwise on the counter. 'I tell you what,' he laughed. 'If you're all that strong, smash this jug in two with your fist, then we'll treat you to as much wine as it contains. But if you can't, the wine's on you.'

My father consented. I stood up, wrapped my handker-chief round my hand and struck. The first two blows had no effect. At the third the jug flew into fragments. 'Pay up!' shouted my father, beaming with delight. The old man ap-peared to have no objection. 'Good,' he said, 'I'll pay for as

much wine as the jug will hold, but it won't be much!'
Naturally the fragments wouldn't hold another measure, but
I had to put up with the chaff, in addition to the pain in my
arm. Even my father laughed at me. 'Well so you've won!'
I shouted, filled the largest fragment from our bottle and
poured it over the old man's head. It was our turn to crow
and we gained a round of applause from the customers.

Further horseplay followed, then my father dragged me off
home, and in a state of peevish excitability we stamped across
the bedroom where, not three weeks before, my mother's
coffin had stood. I slept like the dead and the next morning
I felt a complete wreck. My father jeered at me, was gay and
light-hearted and obviously delighted at his superiority. But
I swore a silent oath never to drink any more and counted
the days before my departure.

Finally it came and I set forth. But I have broken my oath,
for since those days I have become acquainted with the golden
wine of the Vaud, the crimson *Veltliner*, *Neuchâtel* that forms
a star in the glass, not to mention many other wines. And we
have become good friends.

Chapter Three

Once away from the oppressive, humdrum atmosphere of my native village I spread my wings towards bliss and freedom. Though I have often been unlucky in later life, I have richly enjoyed the strange and enchanting delights of youth. Like a young soldier, halted by the green edge of a forest, I lived in blissful restlessness between war and pleasure, and like a seer, full of foreboding, I stood by the sombre chasms, listening to the roar of the mountain torrents and storms, braced to catch the sound of the natural harmonies of all living things. I was happy, I drank deeply from the full cup of youth, silently endured sweet sorrows for the beautiful women whom I worshipped from afar, and tasted to the full the noble joy of friendship. In my new moleskin suit and with my small trunk of books and other possessions, I arrived ready to conquer a piece of the world and to prove as quickly as possible to the rabble at home that I was made of very different stuff from the other Camenzinds.

For three glorious years I lived in the same attic with its draughts and its distant view, studied, wrote verse, hoped, and felt all the beauty of the earth encompass me with its warm presence. It was not every day that I could get a hot meal, but every day, every night and every hour my heart sang, laughed and wept, full of joy. And I clung to this cherished life in a warm, loving embrace.

Zurich was the first large town that I had seen, country bumpkin that I was, and it took me some weeks to get over my amazement. It never occurred to me to admire or even envy city life. In the midst of it all I stared at the impressive buildings and churches; I watched busy people hurrying along to work in great crowds, dawdling students, distinguished inhabitants out for drives, dandies preening themselves, wandering foreign visitors. The vain, smartly-dressed wives of the rich strutted like peacocks in a poultry yard — pretty, proud and faintly grotesque. I was not really shy; merely awkward and defiant and I had no doubt that I was just the man to acquire a thorough knowledge of this exacting city life and that later on I would make myself a secure niche there.

Youth I encountered in the shape of a handsome young man who was studying in the same town and had rented two attractive rooms on the first floor of my house. Every day I heard him playing the piano underneath me, and for the first time in my life I became conscious of the magic of music, the most feminine and sweetest of arts. Then I saw the handsome youth leave the house with a book or sheets of music in his left hand and a cigarette in his right, a trail of smoke curling up behind him as he walked with a light and supple step. Though shyly attracted by him, I kept my distance, fearing to establish any relationship with someone whose ease of manner, grace and prosperity would only make my poverty and lack of *savoir vivre* look ridiculous. But then he approached me himself. One evening there was a knock at my door. I was somewhat frightened as this was the first time anyone had called on me. The handsome student came in, stretched out his hand, and introduced himself in the cheerful, free-and-easy manner of an old acquaintance.

'I wanted to ask you whether you would care to play some music with me,' he said in a friendly voice. But I had never touched a musical instrument in my life. I told him so, adding that my only accomplishment was yodelling, but that I had often listened with pleasure to the enchanting sounds coming up to me from his piano.

'How wrong one can be!' he said cheerfully. 'By the look of you, I could have sworn you were a musician. How odd! But you can yodel? Oh, please yodel, just once! I'd love to hear.'

I was quite taken aback and explained that I couldn't possibly yodel to order, certainly not indoors. It has to be done on a mountain or at least in the open air, and then quite spontaneously.

'Then come and yodel on a mountain! Tomorrow perhaps ? I do implore you to. We could go up together towards evening. We'd wander around and have a chat, then you can yodel. Afterwards we'll have supper in some village. Can you spare the time ?'

Oh, yes, I've time enough, I quickly assented. Then I asked him to play me something and we went down to his large and pleasant living-room. A few pictures in modern frames, the piano, a certain attractive untidiness and the smell of an expensive brand of cigarettes, proclaimed a kind of comfortable elegance, a homely atmosphere which was quite new to me. Richard sat at the piano and played a few bars.

'I expect you know that ?' he said, nodding to me. He looked wonderful as he bent his handsome head towards me with an eager expression in his eyes.

'No,' I replied. 'I'm a complete ignoramus.'

'It's Wagner,' he called back, 'from the *Meistersinger*.' And continued to play. The music had a powerful ease about it; it sounded full of exuberance and longing, and flowed round me like a warm refreshing bath. At the same time I feasted my eyes on the performer's slender neck and back and his white musician's hands. While doing so, I was assailed by the same feeling of admiration and affection as I had felt when in earlier days I had looked at the schoolboy with the chestnut hair. It was mingled with a shy anticipation that this handsome and distinguished being would perhaps really become my friend and thus make my old but not forgotten wish for such a friendship come true.

The next day I called for him. Talking all the time, we slowly climbed a hill, looked down over the town, lake and gardens and savoured to the full the rich beauty of the early evening.

'Now, yodel for me!' said Richard. 'If you still feel shy, turn your back on me! but loudly, please!'

He ought to have been well satisfied for I yodelled madly and exultantly into the glowing evening distance with every possible break and variation. When I stopped he was about to make some remark but suddenly paused, pointed to the mountains and listened. From a distant height came a reply, soft, long-drawn out, then swelling – the greeting of a herdsman or tourist, and we both listened quiet and happy. During this pause I felt a shudder of delight run down my spine at finding myself standing close to a friend for the first time, staring together with him into the alluring remoteness of life ahead of us, overhung with rose-tinged clouds. In the evening light the water of the lake became alive with a soft play of colours and shortly before sunset I observed a few defiant, insolent Alpine peaks surge up from the mist.

'That's where my home is,' I said. 'The middle one is the *Rote Fluh*, on the right is the *Geishorn*, and on the left and farther away the conical *Sennalpstock*. I was ten years and three weeks old the first time I stood on that broad summit.'

I strained my eyes to see another more southerly peak. After a while Richard made a remark which puzzled me.

'What did you say?' I asked.

'I said that I now know what you do.'

'What?'

'You're a poet.'

I blushed and felt put out. At the same time I wondered how he should have guessed.

'No', I cried 'I'm not a poet. I scribbled a few verses at school but I've not written any for ages.'

'May I have a look at them sometime?'

'I've burned them, but I wouldn't let you see them even if I'd still got them!'

'I expect it was very modern stuff with lots of Nietzsche in it!'

'What's that?'

'Nietzsche? Why heavens above, don't you know him?'

'No. How should I?'

He was delighted that I didn't know Nietzsche, but I was

furious and asked him how many glaciers he had crossed. When he replied, 'none', I expressed the same mocking surprise as he had. Then he laid his hand on my arm and said quite seriously, 'You're very touchy. But you don't realize the kind of enviable, unspoilt person you are and how few there are like you. Look, in a year or two you'll know Nietzsche and all the stuff much better than I do, for you are more thorough and intelligent. But I like you as you are at present. You don't know Nietzsche and Wagner but you have been on a lot of snow-mountains and you have such a sturdy mountain face. And you're certainly a poet too. I can see that by your eyes and your forehead.'

I was amazed that he should look at me and express his view with such frankness and absence of embarrassment. It struck me as most unusual. I was even more surprised and delighted when a week later in a much frequented *Biergarten* he swore eternal friendship with me, jumped up and in front of all the customers, kissed me and hugged me, whirling round the table with me as if he was mad.

'What will people think,' I admonished him shyly.

'That these two are either extraordinarily happy or extraordinarily tight! Most of them however, won't give a damn!'

Despite the fact that he was older, more intelligent, better brought up, more subtle and better versed in everything than myself, Richard often seemed a mere child in comparison. In the street, for example, he would flirt in a half-mocking way with young schoolgirls; he would unexpectedly stop playing the most serious piano pieces to make the most childish jokes, and on one occasion when we had gone to church he turned to me suddenly in the middle of the sermon and remarked in a solemn tone, 'Don't you think that the parson looks like a hoary old rabbit?' It was an apt comparison, but I thought he should have kept his remark for afterwards, and I told him so.

'Even though it was a just observation!' he fumed, 'I should probably have forgotten it later.'

His jokes were not always witty; they often depended on

some quotation from *Wilhelm Busch*, but that did not worry me or anybody else, for what we liked and admired in him was not so much his wit and intelligence as the irrepressible gaiety of his childlike, free-and-easy temperament, bursting out every moment and surrounding him with an aura of cheerfulness. It might find an outlet in a gesture, in gentle laughter, in a merry glance; it was certainly never hidden for long. I am convinced that sometimes he must have laughed or made some lighthearted gesture even in his sleep.

Richard brought me into frequent contact with other young people – students, musicians, painters, writers, foreigners from everywhere, for all the interesting and unusual artistic people in the town seemed to swim into his orbit. They included many serious and energetic minds, students of philosophy, aestheticians, socialists. From all these I had a good deal to learn and picked up my knowledge piecemeal from the most varied spheres of life. I supplemented it and read widely as well, gradually gaining some idea of the subjects that tormented and fascinated the liveliest spirits of the day, and what was more, a wholesome and stimulating insight into the cosmopolitan intelligentsia. I found their aims, ambitions, work and ideals attractive and comprehensible, though I was not moved by any strong inner urge to identify myself with any particular group. I noticed that most of them devoted all the energy of their thought and passion to matters concerned with the state of society, politics, science, art, pedagogy; only very few seemed to feel the need to build up their own personalities and to come to terms with life and eternity, regardless of any practical issue. So far, I myself was conscious of this need only intermittently.

I did not make any other friends because of my exclusive and jealous affection for Richard. I even tried to draw him away from women friends with whom he went about a good deal and was on intimate terms. When we arranged to meet, I was always scrupulously punctual however unimportant the event and I was very touchy if he kept me waiting. On one occasion he asked me to call for him at a certain time to go rowing. I went along, but he was out. In vain, I waited three hours for his return. Next day I reproached him bitterly with his neglect.

'Why didn't you go off rowing by yourself then?' he laughed, surprised. 'The whole thing slipped my mind. Surely there's no great harm done?'

'I am accustomed to keep my word scrupulously,' I retorted with some heat, 'but I am also used to your ignoring this fact and keeping me waiting. But of course when one has as many friends as you have . . .'

He looked at me in utter astonishment.

'Heavens above, you do take every trifle to heart!'

'My friendship isn't a trifle to me.'

' "This saying made such deep impress
    That he swiftly swore redress . . .!" '

Richard solemnly quoted, seized hold of my head and rubbed the end of his nose affectionately against mine, orientalwise, and caressed me until I pulled myself away, half-angry half-laughing, but we were friends again.

Modern philosophers, poets, critics – in borrowed, often expensive volumes – literary reviews from Germany and France, new plays, Paris papers and the works of fashionable Viennese critics, all found their way into my attic. But I read these things quickly and gave more purpose and enjoyment to my old Italian story-writers and historical studies. My aim was to abandon languages as soon as possible and to devote myself exclusively to history. Along with works on general history and historical method, I read sources and monographs on the later Middle Ages in France and Italy. It was while thus engaged that I made a close acquaintanceship with my favourite character, that most blessed and godlike of men, St Francis of Assisi. And thus the vision which had given me a glimpse of the fulness of life and of the soul rose before me, becoming more real every day and warming my heart with idealism, joy and youthful conceit. In the lecture room my attention was held by serious, somewhat exacting, and at times tedious scholarship. At home I returned to the comfortably pious or harrowing tales of the Middle Ages or to the leisurely old story-tellers whose beautiful and beneficent world harboured me like a shady, twilight corner in fairyland. At other times, I felt the wild wave of modern ideals and passions sweep over me. I also listened to music, joked with Richard, took part in gatherings with his friends, chatted with Frenchmen, Germans, Russians, heard excerpts read from strange, contemporary books, found my way on occasion to painters' studios or turned up at soirées at which a crowd of excitable and confused young people surrounded me as if at some fantastic carnival.

One Sunday Richard and I went to a small exhibition of new paintings. My friend paused before a picture representing a mountain with some goats on it. It was carefully and neatly executed but in a rather old-fashioned style, and it had no particular artistic merit. One sees plenty of pretty, trivial pictures like this in every salon but it was pleasing to me for its quite faithful rendering of my native pastures. I asked Richard what attracted him about the picture.

'This,' he said pointing to the artist's name in the corner, but I was unable to decipher the dark red signature.

'The picture isn't anything special. There are plenty of more beautiful ones but there isn't a more beautiful woman than the artist. Her name is Erminia Aglietti and if you like we can call on her tomorrow and tell her that she's a great painter.'

'Do you know her?'

'Yes. If her pictures were as beautiful as she is, she would have been rich enough to have stopped painting long ago. In other words, she paints with little enthusiasm, and because she hasn't been taught another way to make a living.'

Richard forgot what he had said and did not refer to it again until a few weeks later.

'I met Erminia Aglietti yesterday. We've been wanting to call on her recently, haven't we, so what about going along now? Have you a clean collar? She notices these things.' My collar was clean and I went with him, not without some misgivings, for the rather unconventional relationships between Richard and his friends with female painters and students had never appealed to me. The men were uncouth, sometimes coarse and sarcastic, the girls practical, clever and shrewd – stripped of the rosy haze through which I liked to see women.

I entered the studio feeling slightly embarrassed. I was already familiar with the general ambience of studios in general, but this was my first visit to a woman's. It looked very bare and tidy. Three or four finished pictures were framed on the walls, another was uncompleted on an easel. The rest of the walls were covered with very neat, intriguing pencil sketches and a half-empty bookcase. Our hostess did not receive us with particular cordiality. She laid down her brush and leaned against the cupboard in her overalls, obviously anxious not to waste much time on us.

Richard extravagantly praised the picture she had been exhibiting. She laughed, not accepting his flattery.

'But Fräulein, I might buy the picture! Anyhow, the cows are so well observed . . .'

'They're goats,' she said calmly.

'Goats? Of course, goats . . . and they show an eye that I find truly amazing. They are really alive, really goatlike. Ask my friend here, Camenzind, who is himself a son of the mountains – he will support me.'

As I listened, half amused, half embarrassed, to the chatter, I could feel the painter's critical glance sweep over me. She looked at me for a considerable time, quite unperturbed.

'So you're from the mountains?'

'Yes.'

'One can see that. Now, what *do* you think of my goats?'

'They're certainly very good. At least, I didn't take them for cows, like Richard.'

'Very good. Are you a musician?'

'No, a student.'

She said nothing more to me and I could now study her at my leisure. Her figure was hidden and distorted by her long overall. Her face did not strike me as beautiful. She had

45

sharp features, her eyes were somewhat severe, her hair abundant, dark and soft. What I found disturbing and unattractive was her complexion. It made me think of gorgonzola cheese, and I wouldn't have been surprised to see green veining in it. I had never come across this southern paleness and by the unflattering morning light of the studio it assumed an alarming pallor – I don't mean like marble but like a very pale, weathered stone. In my boyish way, I was also used to judging a woman's face by its bloom, its pink-and-white complexion and attractiveness rather than by its structure.

Richard was also disappointed with our visit. Thus I was all the more surprised and even alarmed when after a while he told me that Erminia Aglietti would like to draw me. It merely meant a few sketches – she didn't need my face but my broad build apparently had something local about it.

But before anything came of it, another small event occurred that transformed the whole course of my life. One morning I woke up to find I had become a writer. At Richard's instigation I had sketched as accurately as I could and purely as a literary exercise, personalities in our circle, minor events, conversations and so on. I had also written some essays on literary and historical subjects. Richard had come into my room and laid thirty-five francs on my counterpane. 'This belongs to you,' he said in a business-like tone. When I had unsuccessfully racked my brains as to what he meant, he took a newspaper from his pocket in which one of my short stories had been printed. Apparently he had made a copy of several of my manuscripts, taken them along to an editor friend and sold them for me. I was now holding the first piece they had published along with my fee. Never before had my emotions been so mixed. In a way I was annoyed that Richard should have assumed the role of Providence, but the first sweet flush of authorship, the wonderful monetary reward, and the thoughts of minor literary fame finally overcame my irritation.

Richard arranged for me to meet the editor in a café. The editor asked to be allowed to keep the other pieces which Richard had shown him and invited me to submit further contributions. He found an individuality in my writing, especially in the historical essays; he would be glad to receive further contributions and to pay for them in the usual way. I was just beginning to grasp the importance of all this. Not only would I be able to eat regularly and settle my small debts, but very soon I could abandon the studies I had been compelled to follow and work in my chosen field, entirely supported by my own earnings. Meanwhile, at regular intervals, the editor sent me a pile of books for review. I ate my way through them and they kept me busy for weeks. Since my fees were only paid at the end of the quarter however, and I had been living rather more luxuriously on the strength of them, one day I found myself without a penny and once again had to take a 'starvation cure'. I held out for a few days in my attic on a diet of bread and coffee, but then hunger drove me out to a restaurant. I took three review copies along with me to leave as security for my bill. I had already made a vain attempt to sell them at a second-hand bookshop. The meal was excellent but when I reached the coffee stage I began to feel uneasy. With some trepidation I confessed to the waitress that I had no money but wished to leave the books as a pledge. She picked up one of them, a volume of verse, turned over the pages inquisitively and asked if she might read it. She was so fond of reading but could never get hold of any books. I felt saved and suggested that she should accept the three volumes in return for the meal. She agreed, and in this way gradually relieved me of seventeen francs' worth of books. For smaller volumes of verse I claimed bread and cheese, for novels the same food with an addition of wine; individual short stories only brought me a cup of coffee with rolls. As far as I remember, the books were mostly light-weight stuff, couched in an excessively up-to-date idiom, and the good-natured waitress may have gained an extremely odd impression of contemporary German literature. I have a pleasurable recollection of those mornings when I sweated through a volume at great speed, scribbled a few lines about it so that by midday I could exchange it for something to eat. I tried

47

to conceal my poverty from Richard since I was unnecessarily ashamed of it and accepted even occasional help from him with great reluctance.

I did not think of myself as a great poet. What I wrote was magazine verse, not poetry. Inwardly however, I cherished the secret hope that one day I was destined to write real poetry, a daring and ambitious song of life and longing. The bright and cheerful mirror of my soul was clouded at intervals by a kind of melancholy; otherwise it was not seriously troubled. I was overwhelmed sometimes for a day, sometimes a night, by an indefinable loneliness and gloom which vanished without a trace, only to return weeks or months later. In time I became as accustomed to it as a trusted friend until it seemed less of a torment than a disquieting weariness which had its own particular sweetness. When it assailed me at night, instead of sleeping, I lay by the window for hours on end, gazed at the dark waters of the lake, the mountains silhouetted against the pale sky and the lovely stars above them. On such occasions I was often overcome by a tormentingly exquisite sensation as if all this nocturnal loveliness viewed me with justifiable reproach. As if stars, mountains and lake were longing for someone who could understand and voice their beauty and the suffering of their inarticulate existence, as if I were this person whose vocation was to interpret the silence of nature in my poetry. I did not get so far as to consider how I could possibly achieve it. I merely felt the lovely, solemn night waiting impatiently for me with unexpressed longing. Nor in this mood did I ever compose anything. All the same I was aware of a kind of responsibility towards these dark voices, and after such nights I usually took lonely walks that lasted several days. It was, I felt, my way of showing a little affection to the earth which was offering itself to me with dumb entreaties – an idea which caused me to laugh at myself. These journeys became one of the foundations of my later life, for since then I have spent the greater part of my life wandering for weeks or months through many countries. I grew accustomed to walking far afield with little money and a hunk of bread in my pocket, spending entire days in solitude and frequently passing the night in the open. My preoccupation with writing had put Erminia Aglietti completely out of my mind. Then came a note from her. 'I am giving a tea party to friends of both sexes next Thursday. Do come and bring your friend.'

We went along and found a small colony of artists. They were for the most part unrecognized, neglected or unsuccessful. I found this rather pathetic but they all seemed cheerful enough. We were offered tea, bread and butter, ham and salad. As I knew no one there and was reserved by nature, I yielded to my hunger and ate quietly and steadily for about half-an-hour while the others sipped their tea and chatted. When they began to help themselves, it transpired that I had eaten practically all the ham, under the illusion that there was at least another plateful in reserve. As I now became the object of laughter and ironic glances I was furious and inwardly cursed the Italian woman and her ham. I rose to my feet, started hurriedly to leave, explaining to her that another time I would bring my own refreshments. As I reached for my hat, Erminia snatched it and looked at me with quiet astonishment. She implored me to stay. The light from a standard lamp fell on her features and in the midst of my anger I was suddenly struck by her wonderful, mature beauty. I immediately felt extremely stupid and ineffectual and sat down in a far corner of the room like a reprimanded schoolboy. There I remained sitting and turned over the pages of an album with views of Lake Como. The others drank tea, strolled round, laughed and shouted each other down. Somewhere in the background we could hear the tuning of violins and a cello. A curtain was drawn back and we were confronted with four young men seated before improvised music-desks, ready to play a string quartet. At that junction Erminia walked over to me and sat down beside me. The four struck up and went on for a long time, but I heard none of it; I merely stared in wonderment at the slender, delicate, elegantly dressed lady by my side whose beauty I had doubted and whose refreshments I had consumed. With feelings of mixed joy and appre-

4

hension I remembered that she wanted to draw me. Then my thoughts went to Rösi Girtanner, my climb up the mountain-wall for roses, the story of the snow-queen, all of which merely seemed a preparation for the present moment.

When the music was over Erminia did not get up and walk away as I had feared she would but calmly remained seated and began to talk to me. She congratulated me on one of my short stories she had seen in the paper. She joked about Richard, who was the centre of attraction in a group of young girls and whose carefree laughter periodically rose above all the others. She again asked if she might draw me. Then I had an idea. I suddenly switched to Italian, thereby earning not only a look of happy surprise from her vivacious, Mediter-ranean eyes but also experiencing delight at hearing her speak her native tongue, which suited her lips, eyes and physique – the euphonious, rapid *lingua toscana* with a charming sprink-ling of Ticino Swiss. I myself spoke neither well nor fluently, but I was in no way perturbed for the next day I was to be drawn.

'*Arrivederla*' I said as we parted, giving a deep bow.

'*Arrivederci domani.*' She smiled and nodded her assent.

I strode energetically away from her house until the road reached a hill-crest and the dark landscape lay before me in its tranquil, nocturnal repose. A solitary boat with a red lan-tern moved over the lake and threw a few flickering scarlet beams on the black water whose smooth surface was only interrupted by an occasional silvery-edged ripple. In a garden close by, the tremulo of a mandoline rose in the air mingled with the sound of laughter. The sky was almost dark and a strong, warm wind swept over the hill. And as the wind caressed the branches of the fruit-trees and the black tops of the chestnuts, then lashed and bent them so that they moaned, laughed and quivered, it was like an echo of my own violent emotion. I knelt down, lay flat on the earth, jumped up again, groaning, stamped my feet, flung my hat away, buried my face in the grass, shook the tree-trunks, wept, sobbed, raged, again felt ashamed of myself, was happy and then utterly miserable. In an hour's time my whole body became worn out and choked by a fit of dejection. My mind was a blank; I could resolve nothing, feel nothing. I went down the hill as if I was sleep-walking, walked half through the town, saw a small inn that was still open in a side street and entered, in a daze drank a couple of litres of *Waadländer* wine and dragged myself home as dawn broke, terribly drunk.

Next afternoon when I called, Fräulein Aglietti was quite frightened.

'What's wrong with you? Are you ill? You look dreadful.'

'It's nothing much,' I said, 'I think I was very drunk last night that's all. Please make a start!'

She posed me on a chair and asked me to keep still. I did so for I soon became drowsy and slept the whole afternoon in the studio. The dream I had was probably induced by the smell of turpentine; it was about our boat at home. It was being repainted and I was lying on the sandy gravel close by, watching my father pottering round it with a paint brush and paint-pot. My mother was there too and when I asked her whether she wasn't dead, she quietly replied, 'No, for if I wasn't here, you would become a scoundrel like your father.'

In the process of waking up I fell from the chair and was astounded to find myself in Erminia Aglietti's studio. I could not actually see her but I could hear her in the next room, clattering cups and cutlery, and I decided that it must be supper-time.

'Are you awake?' she called over to me.

'Yes. Have I been asleep long?'

'Four hours. Aren't you ashamed of yourself?'

'Yes, but I had such a pleasant dream.'

'Tell me about it.'

'I will if you'll come out and forgive me.'

She came out but would not forgive me until I had recounted my dream. So I told her, and in doing so plunged back into the depths of my forgotten childhood. When eventually I stopped and it was completely dark outside, I had recited the full story of my early days. She gave me her hand, smoothed my ruffled jacket and invited me to come for another sitting the next day. I felt that she had understood and forgiven my unmannerly behaviour.

I sat for her for hours during the next days. We said little to each other. I sat or stood calmly as if spellbound, heard the soft rasp of the charcoal, inhaled the faint smell of oil-paint. My only positive sensation was the feeling of being close to the woman I loved and of knowing that her eyes were continually fixed on me. The pale studio light slid along the walls, a few drowsy flies buzzed over the window-panes and in the small adjacent room the flame of the spirit stove sang, for, after each sitting she gave me a cup of coffee.

At home, my thoughts continued to centre on Erminia. The fact that I was unable to admire her art did not affect or in any way diminish my infatuation. She herself was so beautiful, kindly and self-possessed, what did her paintings matter? There was something about her perseverance; I saw her as a woman battling for a livelihood, a quiet, suffering, courageous heroine. However, there is nothing less rewarding than to think too much about the person one loves. Such trains of thought are like folk and marching songs in which a thousand and one things happen but the refrain recurs with relentless monotony even when it has become totally irrelevant.

Such then is the picture of my handsome Italian painter as it is stored in my memory – not really vague but nevertheless lacking the many little details which we notice much more in strangers than in those nearer to us. For example, I can no longer recall how she did her hair or how she dressed, nor even whether she was tall or small. Whenever I think of her I see a darkhaired, nobly modelled head, not very large eyes set in a pale, animated face, a beautifully shaped, mature and unsensual mouth. I cannot think of her and of my infatuation without recalling the night on the hill with the warm wind blowing over the lake when I wept, almost hysterically happy. And of another evening which I shall now describe.

It was now clear that I must make some kind of confession

to her and declare my love. If we had not been in such close contact I would have been content to worship her from afar and to suffer in silence. But as things were, seeing her, entering her house with my heart in a state of torment, I could not restrain myself for long. A summer party had been arranged for artists and their friends. It took place by the lake in a pretty garden. The still water received the oars with a gentle gurgle; other boats floated here and there, darkly, hardly visible on the calm surface, but I gave them little attention for my eyes were fixed steadfastly on the steerer, and my intended declaration of love weighed on my timid heart like a heavy iron ring. The beauty and poetry of the evening as we sat in the boat, the stars, the warm and tranquil lake – everything overawed me, so closely did it resemble a theatrical décor before which I had to act a sentimental scene. Fearful and numbed by the profound stillness – for neither of us spoke – I rowed as hard as I could.

'How strong you are!' she remarked pensively.

'Fat, don't you mean?' I said.

'No. I mean muscular,' she laughed.

'Yes. I am strong.'

It was not an auspicious opening. Depressed and irritated, I continued to row. After a while I asked her to tell me something about her life.

'What sort of thing do you want to hear?'

'Everything,' I said. 'Preferably a love story. Then I'll tell you one of mine – my only one in fact. It's very short and sweet, and it will amuse you!'

'Fancy that! Go ahead.'

'No, you first! You already know much more about me than I about you. I would like to know if you have ever really been in love, or whether – as I suspect – you are too clever and proud!'

Erminia pondered a moment.

'That's just one of your romantic notions,' she said. 'Listening to a woman talking about her past here at night on the dark water. But I'm afraid I can't oblige. You poets have pretty words for everything and consider those who don't flaunt their emotions as heartless. You have been mistaken about me, for I do not think anyone could be capable of a stronger and deeper love than I. I love a man who is tied to another woman and who also loves me. Yet neither of us knows whether it will ever be possible for us to come together. We write and meet at intervals. . .'

'May I ask whether this love brings you happiness or only distress ? Or both ?'

'Alas, love doesn't exist to make us happy. I believe it exists to show us how steadfast we can be in sorrow and endurance.'

That at least I could understand, and I was unable to repress the faint moan which escaped my lips in reply. She heard it.

'Ah,' she said. 'You too are aware of it ? But you're still so young. Do you want to tell me about it ? Only if you really want to . . .'

'Another time perhaps, Signorina Aglietti. Anyway, I feel too shaken today. I'm afraid that perhaps I have spoilt your evening too.'

'As you wish. How far are we from the shore ?'

I did not reply. I pressed the oars against the water with a splash, swung the boat round and pulled as though a Northeaster was getting up. The boat moved swiftly over the surface and in all the confusion of anguish and mortification which seethed inside me, I felt the perspiration run down my face in great drops and yet I felt very cold. When I realized how near I had been to playing the suitor on his knees, the lover rejected with motherly understanding, a shudder ran down my spine. At least I had been spared that, and now it was a matter of coming to terms with the aftermath of my distress. I rowed homeward like one possessed.

The beautiful Signorina was somewhat taken aback when, on reaching the bank, I left her hurriedly standing alone. The lake was smooth, the music as gay and the Chinese lanterns as festively red as before, but now everything seemed stupid and meaningless. Especially the music. I felt I could have beaten to a jelly the student in the velvet cloak who still brandished his guitar in its broad silk sling. And there were fireworks to come. How childish it all was!

I borrowed a few francs from Richard, rammed my hat on the back of my head and started out from the outskirts of the town, walking mile after mile until exhausted. I lay down in a field only to wake an hour later, soaked to the skin from the dew, stiff and half-frozen, and walked on to the next village. It was early morning. Reapers on their way to mow the clover were strolling through the dusty streets, drowsy farm labourers stared at me from stable doors, summer farming activities were everywhere in evidence. You should have remained a peasant, I said to myself as I strode on through the village, shamefaced, hurrying on until the first warmth of the sun allowed me to halt. At the edge of a beech-grove I threw myself down on the grass between two fields and slept in the hot sun until late afternoon. When I woke with my head full of the scent of the grass and my limbs agreeably tired, as they can only be after lying for a long time on God's good earth, the festivities, the trip on the lake and the whole affair already seemed remote, sad and half-forgotten like a novel one has read months before.

I stayed away for three whole days, letting the sun tan my skin while I considered whether or not to go home straightaway and help my father with the second crop of hay. Naturally it was a long time before I recovered from my distress. When I returned I started by avoiding my painter like the plague, but that phase soon passed and every time she looked at me or spoke, I felt a choking sensation in my throat.

Chapter Four

Disappointment in love achieved something that had been beyond my father's powers – it drove me to drink. The effect was more far-reaching than anything I have so far mentioned in this narrative. The strong, sweet god of wine became my true friend – as he remains even today. With whom can he effectively be compared? Who is more handsome, whimsical, exuberant, cheerful and melancholy? He is both hero and magician, tempter and brother of Eros. He can accomplish the impossible; he fills poor human hearts with beautiful and splendid poetry. He transformed me from the hermit and peasant I was into a king, poet and sage. He fills the emptied vessels of life with new destinies and sweeps those who are beached back into the swift main current.

Such is the nature of wine. Yet as with all precious gifts and arts, it must be sought out and cherished, understood and subdued by great effort. Few can accomplish this and so the god brings destruction upon thousands. He ages them, kills them or extinguishes the flame of the spirit. His favourites however he invites to his banquets, builds them rainbow-bridges to the Isles of the Blessed. When they are weary he lays pillows under their heads and embraces them, and when they fall prey to sorrow, he clasps them gently in his arms like a comforting mother. He transforms the confusion of life into great myths, and plays the hymn of creation on his mighty harp.

Other times he assumes child-like form with long silky curls, narrow shoulders and slender limbs. He nestles against your heart and raises his narrow face up towards yours and gazes at you dreamily from loving, inquiring eyes in whose depths memories of paradise lost and rediscovered innocence gush forth, sparkling like a fresh spring in the forest. And the sweet god is also like a deep, rushing stream journeying through a springtime night; and like a sea that cradles the sun and storm on its cool waves. When he converses with his chosen ones, the storm-tide of secrets, memories, poetry, and longings pours over them. The known world shrinks and fades away, and the soul hurls itself with trembling joy into the unchartered void of the unknown where everything is strange yet familiar and where the language of music, poets and dreams is spoken.

But I must return to my story. At times I found it possible to forget myself and be light-hearted for hours at a stretch. I pursued my studies, wrote and listened to Richard's music. But no day passed without an ache in my heart. Sometimes it only attacked me in bed at night and then I moaned aloud, sat up and finally sobbed myself to sleep. Or it returned after a meeting with Signorina Aglietti. Mostly, however, it happened in late afternoons when the warm, enervating summer evenings began. On these occasions I went to the lake, took a boat, rowed until I was hot and exhausted, then found it impossible to return home. I went to a tavern where I sampled various wines, drank, brooded and felt ill next day. A dozen times I fell victim to such terrible depression and nausea that I resolved to give up drinking. But then I would start again. Gradually I learned to distinguish between the different wines and gauge their effects on me and I began to enjoy them with a certain expertise, though, I must admit in a rather ingenuous and elementary manner. Finally, I decided in favour of dark red Veltliner. My first glass had a certain exciting sharpness, then clouded my thoughts which became calm and dreamy. As I continued to drink, it cast a spell over me and composed its own poetry. Through its fumes I described all the landscapes that had ever enchanted me; they enveloped me in a kind of magic light, and I strode into them, sang, dreamed and had the feeling that a warm, heightened existence hovered around me. I would end in a mood of exquisite melancholy;

it was if I had heard the sound of ancient folk-songs played on fiddles and that somewhere close by great happiness lay in wait for me that I had wandered past and overlooked.

Without any deliberate attempt, it happened that I drank less on my own and less frequently and found myself in all kinds of mixed company. Once I had kindred spirits round me, the wine affected me in a different way; I became talkative without getting excited; it was like suffering from a strange, cold fever. A new side of my personality – one of which I had so far hardly been aware – blossomed overnight, but it belonged more to the world of thistles and nettles than to garden flowers. As I became more eloquent, a cool, sharp spirit would pass over me, making me self-possessed, patronizing, critical and witty. If there were people present of whom I disapproved, I drove them away with subtle witticisms or coarse sallies. From childhood days I had never found my fellow-creatures particularly endearing or indispensable, and I now began to examine them with critical irony. Above all, I enjoyed inventing and telling little stories in which the relations between human beings were presented with a cold-blooded, matter-of-factness and withering scorn. I could not think why I did it. It just erupted from my system like a ripening abscess which took me many years to shake off. If occasionally I was alone in the evening, I still dreamed of mountains, stars and melancholy music.

During those weeks I wrote a series of articles about the society, culture and art of our time, and composed a venomous little book, the fruits of my conversations in the local inn. They were supplemented by a number of historical pieces based on my fairly assiduous historical research, which provided some sort of solid background to my satires. On the strength of this work I was appointed as a permanent contributor to a quite important newspaper, and could almost support myself on the proceeds of my work. The articles were published immediately afterwards in book form and enjoyed some success. I now threw my studies completely overboard. By this time I had had some years at the university, and had made contacts with certain German periodicals. This elevated me from my previous obscurity into the circle of recognized authors. I earned my own living, gave up my tiresome bursary and was rapidly heading towards the unenviable life of a minor professional man-of-letters.

But despite this success and my conceit, despite the satires and my unhappy love-affair, the warm glow of youth never left me in my happiness and distress. Despite my cynicism and mild sophistication, I still kept an aim in my thoughts, a target of happiness and self-fulfilment. I had no idea what form it would take. All I felt was that life was bound to spill some wonderful piece of luck at my feet, fame of some kind, love perhaps, a satisfaction of my longing and a heightening of my being. I was still very much the page dreaming of noble ladies, of knighthood and great honours. I believed that I had my foot at the starting-point of a rising slope. I failed to realize that everything I had so far experienced consisted of chance happenings, and that my way of life still lacked the kind of yearning that neither love nor fame can satisfy or circumscribe. And so I enjoyed my petty, somewhat crude success with all the ebullience of youth. It felt good to be in the company of witty and intellectual men with a glass of wine before me and to watch their eyes turn eagerly and attentively in my direction when I spoke.

Sometimes I was struck by the tremendous craving of my generation for a solution to their problems and the odd paths they were led along. It was considered stupid, almost indecent to believe in God, but other teachings and names – Schopenhauer, Buddha, Zarathustra to quote a few – won wide acceptance. There were young anonymous poets who did their solemn devotions before statues and paintings in their modish houses. They would have been ashamed to bow before God but knelt before the Zeus of Otricoli. There were ascetics who suffered tortures from their abstinence and went round looking like scarecrows. *Their* god was Tolstoy or Buddha. There were artists who sought access to a more rarefied atmosphere through the medium of exquisite wallpapers, music, gastronomy, wines, perfumes and cigars. They discoursed eloquently on melodic line, colour harmony, and such like and were always on the look-out for the 'individual touch' which consisted for the most part in some small, harmless self-deception or eccentricity. I found their entire unnatural spectacle grotesque and ridiculous, but this did not prevent me realizing, with an awed shudder, how much serious aspiration and true strength of mind flared up in this way, only to burn itself out.

Among all the posturing crows of fashionable poets, artists and philosophers whom I was then delighted and dazzled to meet, not one achieved any real fame. There was a North German of my age, an agreeable person, delicate and attractive, refined and sensitive in all cultural matters. He was considered one of the great coming poets and some of his poems that I heard still have, as I remember them today, rare fragrance and an ethereal beauty. Perhaps he was the only one among us who had the makings of true poet. Later on, I chanced to hear something of his brief story. This hypersensitive soul lost confidence through lack of literary success, had withdrawn from social activity and had fallen into the hands of an unscrupulous patron who, far from providing encouragement and sound advice, had brought about his ruin. The poet indulged in pseudo-aesthetic conversations in the villas belonging to his patron among a bevy of female hangers-on, looked upon himself as a kind of misunderstood hero, and as a result of a continual overdose of Chopin and Pre-Raphaelite aestheticism, systematically destroyed his reason. I cannot without feelings of distress and sympathy, think back to that half-baked assortment of eccentrically-dressed, curly-haired poets and rarefied souls, for it was only later on that I perceived the dangers that lurked within such circles. At that stage it had been my highland peasant nature that came to my rescue and stopped me contending in the lists.

Nobler and more rewarding than fame, wine, love and wisdom was my friendship. That alone came to the rescue of my innate melancholy and kept my youthful years fresh, unspoilt and glowing like the dawn. Even today I can think of nothing more precious that a strong, firm friendship between men, and if in more pensive moments I succumb to anything like nostalgia, it is only for my student friendships.

Since my infatuation with Erminia I had neglected Richard. At first I was unaware of this, but after some weeks my conscience smote me. I made my confession; he told me that he had watched the progress of the whole unfortunate business with considerable distress, but that I could now reassume my old relationship sincerely and unreservedly. Whatever I now acquired of the happy and liberal minor pleasures of life I owed to him. He was handsome and exuberant in mind and body; life seemed to cast no shadows for him. An intelligent and lively person, he was under no illusion about the passions and errors of our time, but they slid harmlessly off him. His gait, speech, his whole being was resilient, light-hearted and amiable. How he could laugh! He showed little appreciation of my wine researches. He sometimes accompanied me to an inn, but two glasses of wine always sufficed and he regarded my much greater consumption with naive astonishment. But when he saw that I was a helpless victim of fits of melancholy, he would play or read to me and take me for walks. On these expeditions we often became as boisterous as schoolboys. On one occasion, when having a siesta in a wooded valley, we pelted each other with pine-cones and sang ribald verses to soulful tunes. The clear, swift stream splashed cool and inviting in our ears while we stripped and lay in the cold water. Then we began to play the fool. He perched himself on a moss-grown rock pretending to be Lorelei and I sailed past below – the sailor in his little boat. He looked so girlish and demure and pulled such faces that I, who was supposed to be consumed with the 'wildest woe', could hardly contain my laughter. Suddenly we heard voices. A group of tourists appeared on the path and we had to hide our nakedness with great alacrity under a hollow place where the river bank had been worn away, while the company strode past in blissful ignorance. Richard made a series of weird noises, grunts, squeaks and hisses. The tourists stopped, looked round, stared into the water and nearly discovered us. Then Richard half raised himself from the hole, looked at the indignant company, assumed a priestlike bearing, and cried in deep, resonant tones 'Go your way in peace!' and immediately ducked down again. He pinched my arm. 'That was a charade too,' he said.

'What did it represent?' I asked.

'Pan startling the shepherds,' he laughed, 'but unfortunately there were some women among them!'

Richard showed little interest in my historical studies. But he soon shared my passion for St Francis of Assisi, although he was capable of making jokes about him that made me angry. We followed the patient saint as he wandered through the Umbrian landscape, gay and loving as a child, rejoicing in his God and full of compassion for all men. Together we read his immortal Hymn to the Sun, and knew it almost off by heart. Once, when we were returning home from an expedition by a steamer on the lake and the evening breeze was ruffling the golden water, he quietly asked, 'What does the Saint say about this?' And I quoted:

'*Laudato sì, misignore, per frate vento et per aere et nubilo et sereno et onne tempo!*'

When we quarrelled and cursed each other, he hurled such a host of fantastic names at me, always half in jest like a schoolboy, that I couldn't help laughing, and the sting was taken from the quarrel. Richard was relatively serious only when listening to his favourite composers, or playing their works. Even then he would break off to make some quip. Yet his love for music was full of pure, sincere reverence and he seemed to me to have an unerring feeling for the genuine and significant. He also had a wonderful understanding of the tender act of comforting and sympathetic sharing of sorrow whenever one of his friends was in trouble. When he found me in a cross mood he could relate countless grotesquely amusing anecdotes, and there was something cheering and enlivening about his manner of telling them which I found irresistible.

He showed a certain respect for me because I was more serious, and my physique impressed him still more. He sang my praises in front of other people, and was proud to have a friend who could have strangled him with one hand. He set great store by physical prowess. He taught me tennis, rowed and swam with me, took me riding and was not satisfied until I could play billiards as skilfully as he. It was his favourite game. He practised it with art and mastery, and seemed particularly lively, witty and cheerful when playing it. He would often dub the three balls with names of acquaintances and at every stroke of the cue fabricated whole stories, full of wit, satire and caricature, according to the relative position of the balls. Yet this did not interfere with his calm, casual stylish game which it was a pleasure to watch.

He set no more store by my writing than I did. Once he said to me, 'Look, I once thought of you as a poet and I still do so, not on the strength of your newspaper contributions but because I feel that you have something fine and profound in your life which sooner or later will come to light. Whatever it turns out to be, it will be true poetry.'

Meantime the university terms slipped by like small coins between the fingers, and all of a sudden we were confronted with the moment when Richard had to think of returning to his home. We savoured the fleeting weeks with a somewhat artificial heartiness and both agreed that we should wind up these wonderful years in a gay and worthwhile manner with some brilliant and festive undertaking before our sad final goodbye. I suggested a holiday tour in the Bernese Oberland, but Spring had not yet come, and it was much too early for the mountains. While I racked my brains for other ideas, Richard wrote to his father and secretly prepared a great and splendid surprise. One day he arrived with a fat cheque and invited me to accompany him to Northern Italy as a guide. My heart beat with feelings of mixed apprehension and joy. A wish that I had cherished since childhood, a longing that was very close to my heart and had been the subject of a hundred dreams was about to be fulfilled. I feverishly set about my modest preparations, supplied Richard with a few Italian phrases and was in a panic to the very last minute for fear our plans should come to nothing.

Our luggage was sent on in advance and we sat in the carriage. The green meadows and hills slid by, the Urnersee and the St Gothard tunnel approached, then the little mountain villages, the streams and boulder-strewn slopes and snow-peaks of the Ticino, followed by the first stone houses in flat vineyards and the last lap, full of expectation, past the Italian lakes, and over the fertile plains of Lombardy towards the oddly attractive and repellent city of Milan with its strident vigour.

Richard had never formed a picture of Milan Cathedral in his mind, having merely known it as a famous masterpiece of architecture. His indignant disillusionment was highly a-musing. When he had recovered from his initial shock and had regained his good humour, he proposed to climb onto the roof and stroll round among the fantastic array of stone figures up there. With a certain satisfaction we discovered that we needn't have been so disillusioned after all, since most of the hundreds of wretched statues of saints on the pinnacles, and all the more modern ones, turned out to be the usual kind of machine-made products. We lay almost two hours on the wide, sloping marble roof which was warmed by a mild April sun. As he lay there stretched at ease, Richard confessed, 'You know I wouldn't mind experiencing more disappointments like this with this fantastic cathedral. I was slightly apprehensive that we might be overwhelmed by all the "sights" we should see on our tour, and now it starts off in this amiable and humanly ridiculous way.' Then the population of stone statues among which we lay inspired him to indulge in all kinds of weird extravagancies.

'I presume,' he began, 'that that one on the tower above the choir, which is the loftiest point of the building, must be the loftiest and most superior saint. As it cannot be much fun to balance on these pointed pinnacles, it is only reasonable that from time to time the loftiest saint should be relieved and taken up to heaven. Just imagine what a fuss that must cause every time it happens! For naturally each of the remaining saints will move up a place and each one will have to shift in a single leap to the pinnacle occupied by his predecessor — every one of them in a terrific hurry and full of jealousy of all the others who go in front of him.'

Whenever I have passed through Milan since, I have re-called that afternoon and I have imagined those hundreds of marble saints doing their bold leaps and I have smiled a melancholy smile.

In Genoa I gathered another rich experience. It was a bright, windy day in the afternoon. I was leaning my elbows on a broad parapet. Behind me lay the many-coloured town and below stretched the blue, living water of the sea. With sinister roars and vague yearning the eternal, immutable ele-ment hurled itself towards me and I felt something within me had made an eternal friendship with those blue, foam-flecked waters.

The far-off horizon impressed me no less. Once again as in childhood, I saw the soft blue distance inviting me like an open door. And once again I was overcome by the feeling that I was not born for the life of a perpetual stay-at-home among my fellow men in towns and houses, but for pilgrimages through foreign lands and journeys over the sea. I felt the old melancholy impulse to fling myself on God's breast and merge my own insignificant life into the infinite and eternal.

At Rapallo I enjoyed my first battle with the sea, tasted the tang of salt-water and felt the power of the waves. Clear, blue waves all round me, golden cliffs, a deep tranquil sky and the perpetual pounding of the sea. I was continually gripped by the sight of the distant gliding ships, the black masts and white sails or the ribbon of smoke of a steamer as it moved away. Next to my beloved clouds and their shifting glory, I know no finer or more impressive symbol of man's yearning and pilgrimage than a ship dwindling in the distance and finally disappearing on the open sky-line.

We arrived in Florence. The town lay there just as I had

imagined it from scores of pictures and hundreds of dreams — light, spacious, welcoming, traversed by its green river with its many bridges and surrounded by sunlit hills. The bold tower of the Palazzo Vecchio rose defiantly against the cloudless sky. On the high ground beyond, white and warm in the sunshine lay lovely Fiesole, and all the hills were pink and white in the full flower of the fruit-blossom season. The gay, innocent life of Tuscany rose up miraculously before me and I felt more at home there than I had ever felt on my native heath. And so we idled away the days in churches, piazzas, narrow streets, arcades and markets, and dreamed the evenings away in hill-gardens where the lemons were already ripening or drank and talked in small simple wineshops. And in between were rewarding hours spent in the picture galleries and the Bargello, the monasteries, libraries and sacristies; afternoons in Fiesole, San Miniato, Settignano, Prato.

In accordance with a plan previously agreed on I now left Richard for a week and enjoyed the finest and most precious journey of my youth through the rich, green Umbrian hill country. I followed the roads once trodden by St Francis and often had the feeling that he was wandering beside me, his heart, like mine, filled with an unfathomable love for all God's creatures, greeting every bird, every Spring and every dog-rose with joy and gratitude. I plucked and ate lemons on bright, sunny hillsides, spent the nights in small villages, sang and wrote verse for my own amusement and celebrated Easter in Assisi in my Saint's own church.

I still feel that week's journey in Umbria was the crown and also the glorious sunset of my youth. Each day new sources welled up within me and I gazed into the light, gay Spring landscape as if I was looking into the loving eyes of God himself.

In Umbria I humbly followed the steps of St Francis, the musician of God; in Florence I basked in the permanent revelation of the quattrocento. I had already composed satires at home on contemporary life, but it was in Florence that I first became conscious of the threadbare stupidity of modern culture. It was there too that I was overcome for the first time by the feeling that I would always be a stranger in our modern society, and the impulse first awoke in me to lead my life outside it, if possible in the south. There I could talk with people and savour a natural, unspoilt life which had been ennobled and refined by the tradition of its classical and past culture.

Brilliant and happy, those wonderful weeks went by. I had never seen even Richard so completely enraptured. Exuberant and cheerful we drained the cup of beauty and joyfulness. We wandered through out-of-the-way, sunlit mountain hamlets, made friends with innkeepers, monks, country girls and unassuming village priests; listened to native serenades, offered food and fruit to dark, pretty children, and from sunny mountain-tops looked down on Tuscany in the brightness of Spring and the Ligurian Sea shimmering in the distance. We both had the inescapable sensation of approaching a rich, new life, worthy of our destiny. Work, struggle, enjoyment and fame lay so near, so effulgent, so much within our grasp that we felt able to savour those blissful days without undue haste. We were even reconciled to our separation which would only be provisional, for we knew now with ever-deepening certainty that we were indispensable to each other and could depend on each other for the rest of our lives.

That is the story of my youth. As I think back, it seems as brief as a summer night. A little music, wit, love, conceit – but lovely, rich and colourful withal as an Eleusinian feast.

And it was snuffed out as quickly and miserably as a candle in the wind.

Richard left me in Zurich. Twice he got out of the railway compartment to embrace me, and nodded his head affectionately from the window as the train went out. Two weeks later he was drowned while bathing in a ridiculously small river in South Germany. I never set eyes on his face again. I was not present at his funeral, and news of it reached me only when it was all over and his coffin was already in the ground. I flung myself down in my small attic room, wept, raged, and cursed God and life in cheap and portentous imprecations. I had not before realized that my only sure possession in those years had been my friendship. Now it was past and gone.

I could not bear to stay any longer in the town where a host of memories crowded in on me and choked me. I no longer cared what happened. I was sick at heart and every aspect of life was repellent to me. For the time being there seemed little prospect that my broken life would ever be mended and ride with newly hoisted sails towards the rougher happiness of manhood. God had decreed that I should surrender the best of my being to a joyful and unclouded friendship. We had come together like two swiftly moving skiffs. Richard's boat was the gay, happy-go-lucky one on which my eyes had been fixed and which I confidently hoped would bear me along to my glorious destination. But with a short cry it had sunk, and now I, rudderless, was tossed around on waters that had all at once become dark.

I should now have addressed myself to the hard test of navigation by the stars and battling my way on a new voyage to wrest the crown of life. I had believed in friendship, in woman's love and in youth. These things had abandoned me in turn. Why did I not trust in God and surrender myself to his stronger arms? But all my life I have been as timid and as obstinate as a child. I was always waiting for my real life to take me by storm, make me rich and wise and bear me on its great wings towards some more adult happiness. But life in its wisdom quietly allowed me to go on. It sent me neither storms nor stars, but waited until I regained my patience and humility, and my pride was broken. It let me play out my comedy of pride and priggishness and watched and waited for the truant child to find its mother again.

Chapter Five

I now come to that period of my life which was outwardly more animated and cheerful than any other that preceded it, and which at the best could form the basis of a slight, popular novel. At this point I should describe how I was appointed editor of a German newspaper, indulged my pen and malicious tongue too freely, paid the penalty and was brought back to heel for my pains. How next I began to drink and ended by involving myself in a shady business, gave up my job and got myself posted to Paris as a special correspondent. How I subsequently wasted my time in that pernicious spot, wasted my time and played fast and loose in all sorts of ways.

If I skip that brief period in my life and cheat the more sordid among my potential readers it must not be attributed to cowardice on my part. I am prepared to admit that I took one wrong path after another, waded in every kind of pitch and did not escape undefiled. Since then I have lost my enthusiasm for the 'romantic' and bohemian life, and you must allow me to deal with the better and more wholesome aspects of my past and reject and forget the wasted years.

One evening I was sitting alone in the Bois de Boulogne wondering whether to leave Paris and even life itself. Thus preoccupied, I reviewed my past history for the first time and concluded that I had little to lose. But then the recollection of a long forgotten day suddenly returned to my mind. It was a morning in early summer in my mountain village and I saw myself kneeling by a bed on which my mother lay dying. I was overcome with panic and felt ashamed that I had allowed the memory of that morning slip from my mind for so long. My stupid contemplations of suicide were over, for I am sure that no man in his senses ever considered taking his own life once he has witnessed the extinction of another's healthy and good life. Once more I had the vision of my dying mother. I saw the grim, silent work of death on her face and the dignity it lent her. Death looked stern enough but at the same time it was the mighty and kindly father bringing home an erring child. Once more I suddenly realized that death is a wise and good brother who knows the right moment and on whom we can confidently depend. I began to understand that sorrow, disappointments and sadness do not exist to distress us, to make us worthless and undignified, but rather to bring us to a full state of maturity and enlightenment.

A week later my boxes were despatched to Basel, and I set off on foot through an enchanting region in the South of France, every day more conscious that my unhealthy period in Paris, the memory of which clung to me like a foul smell, was gradually melting away. My life became like an attendance at a medieval Court of Love. I spent the night in castles, mills, barns and in the company of dark and loquacious peasants drank their warm, sunny wine.

Lean, sunburnt, my clothes the worse for wear, inwardly transformed, I arrived at Basel two months later. It had been my first extensive journey but the first of many. There are few places between Locarno and Verona, Basel and Brig, Florence and Perugia through which I have not made two or three journeys in dusty boots, pursuing dreams, none of which has yet been fulfilled.

In Basel I rented lodgings in a suburb, unpacked my belongings and began to work. I was glad to live in a quiet town where I was unknown. I still had connections with some newspapers and reviews and had enough to do and enough to live on. The first few weeks went well and uneventfully, then gradually I fell a victim to the old depression which persisted for days and weeks and which even work failed to dispel. No one who has not suffered from fits of depression can understand. How shall I describe the state I was in? I was conscious of a sensation of terrifying loneliness. Between me and other men and the life of the town, the squares, houses and streets stretched a broad, unbridgeable gulf. A great tragedy might occur, important events appear in the newspapers but they did not touch me. Festivities were celebrated, dead were buried, markets held, concerts given – what meaning had they for me? I escaped, fled to the woods, the mountains, the roads and all round me were the silent meadows, trees, fields, dumb witnesses gazing at me in silent entreaty as if they yearned to convey some message, approach and greet me. But they were inarticulate, and I understood their sufferings in sympathy for I could not save them.

I considered a doctor, set down my case history in writing, and tried to describe my complaint. He read my notes, questioned and examined me.

'You are enjoying enviably good health,' he said. 'Physically there is nothing wrong with you. Try and cheer yourself up with books and music.'

'My profession requires me to read a lot of new things every day.'

'At any rate you could treat yourself to some walks in the open air.'

'I walk three to four hours every day and in holiday time twice that amount.'

'Then you must force yourself to seek company. You're in danger of becoming a recluse.'

'What does that matter?'

'It matters a lot. The greater your distaste for company is now, the more you must compel yourself to mix with your fellow-men. Your condition cannot be described as pathological so far, nor does it seem serious, but if you continue going around so aimlessly, your balance of mind may well be disturbed in the end.'

The doctor was a kindly and understanding man. He was sorry for me. He recommended me to a scholar whose house could be described as a centre of intellectual and literary life.

I went along. They knew my name, and were kind, almost cordial, and I often repeated my visits.

On one occasion there – it was a chilly late autumn evening – I met a young historian and a very slim, dark girl. There were no other guests. The girl made the tea, talked a good deal and was witty at the expense of the historian. Later, she played the piano for a short while. Then she mentioned having read, but not enjoyed my satires. She gave me the impression of being clever, perhaps too clever, and I soon went off home.

Meantime it had gradually got around that I spent too much time in taverns and was also a solitary drinker. I was not surprised, for it was precisely in this mixed academic circle that scandal flourished most. The humiliating disclosure had little effect on my social relations, on the contrary it caused me to be much in demand, since there was a great deal of enthusiasm for the temperance cause. Both men and women belonged to committees of various temperance societies and rejoiced over every sinner who fell into their hands. One day, the first polite onset began. The disgrace involved in frequenting taverns, the curse of alcoholism, all this viewed from the hygienic, ethical and social stand-point, was thrust under my nose, and I was invited to attend a temperance club soirée. It was an astonishing experience. Hitherto I had known almost nothing about clubs and movements of that kind. The session with its music and atmosphere of uplift was painfully comic and I made no attempt to hide my reactions. For weeks afterwards I was importuned with pressing amiability; the whole business became extremely boring, and one evening when they had kept harping on the same theme and expressed urgent hopes of my conversion, I became desperate and begged them to spare me their tirades. The dark girl was there again. She listened to me attentively and said 'Hear hear!' However, I was too annoyed to pay much attention.

Therefore I derived all the more pleasure from witnessing an untoward incident which took place at an important temperance rally. The vast society and their numerous guests had met for a banquet at their headquarters. Speeches were made, friendships struck up, hymns sung, and the progress of the great cause celebrated with much rejoicing. One of the attendants, appointed as banner-bearer, found the speeches too tedious to bear and went off to a nearby tavern, and when the solemn procession and demonstration started through the streets, malicious sinners enjoyed the diverting spectacle of a cheerfully drunken leader bearing the banner of the Blue Cross swaying in his arms like the mast of a wrecked ship.

They rid themselves of the intoxicated attendant but not of the innumerable vanities, petty jealousies and intrigues which had arisen within the individual rival clubs and societies and continued to prosper and abound. There was a schism within the movement; a section of the more ambitious members wanted all the glory for themselves, and every drunken reprobate who was reclaimed other than in their name, they took as a slight to themselves. Respectable and unselfish collaborators, of whom there were plenty, were treated with scorn. Soon disinterested onlookers had the opportunity of seeing how, even under an idealistic label, all kinds of undesirable human frailties could smell to high heaven. I learned about these comic activities from third party sources and derived a quiet satisfaction from them, and as I returned from my not infrequent night-sprees I reflected 'Behold, we wilder spirits are after all no worse than you!'

I pursued my studies and research assiduously in my little room overlooking the Rhine. It was a cause of deep distress to me as I wathed life flowing past me that I never seemed to be caught up by any current. No devouring passion or enthusiasm claimed me or snatched me from my idle dreams. It is true that over and above my daily tasks I was preparng a book on the lives of the early Minorites, but it was not an original work, merely a patient and modest composition that by no means satisfied my creative urge. While my memories of Zurich, Berlin and Paris were still fresh I began to grasp the aspirations, passions and ideas of my contemporaries. One of them had set himself the task of persuading people to discard the outmoded furniture, wall-paper designs and fashions of the past and to introduce them to a freer and more beautiful environment. Another was engaged in propaganda for Haeckel Monism by means of popular writings and lectures. Others put all their efforts in working for permanent and universal peace. Another was fighting for the starving underdogs or speaking at mass meetings on behalf of schemes to build and inaugurate People's theatres and art-galleries. And here in Basel they were combating alcoholism.

All these good works had drive and vigour behind them. Yet no cause seemed important or necessary to me, and it would not have affected my life one whit if all the aims mentioned had been attained. Despairingly I sank back into my chair, pushed my books and papers to one side and pondered. At that point I heard the Rhine rushing by, the wind howling, and I listened, fascinated, to the language, of this great longing and melancholy which seemed to lie in perpetual ambush. I watched the pale clouds of night swooping like frightened birds across the sky, heard the Rhine and thought of my mother's death, of St Francis, of my home among the snow-covered mountains, of poor, drowned Richard. I saw myself climbing the cliff walls again to pluck Alpine roses for Rösi Girtanner, and in Zurich, intoxicated by literature, music and conversation. I saw myself rowing on the twilight lake water with Erminia, and in despair over Richard's death, travelling, returning, cured, then suffering again. All for what purpose? To what end? O God, had it all been a game then, chance, a painted picture? Had I not striven and suffered torture in my quest for the spirit, friendship and beauty? Did not the warm waves of love and longing still well up inside me? And all to no purpose; merely for my own torment and bringing no joy to anyone! It was at such moments that the tavern claimed me. I would blow out the light, grope my way down the steep old winding stairway and go into some wine shop where they sold Veltliner or Vaud wine. There I was received with respect as a good customer but my behaviour was usually defiant and sometimes exceedingly rude. I read *Simplizissmus* which never failed to infuriate me, drank my wine and waited to feel its effects. Then the sweet god would touch me with a soft, feminine hand, induce an agreeable weariness into my limbs and lead my lost soul to the land of the beautiful dreams.

Sometimes my boorish treatment of other people and the amusement I derived from making fun of them surprised even me. At the inns which I frequented, the waitresses feared and cursed me as a mannerless grumbler with a perpetual grievance. If I got into conversation with other customers, I became coarse and scornful; people seemed to expect this of me. Nevertheless I managed to keep a few drinking companions, all of them elderly reprobates with whom I sometimes spent an evening and was on tolerable terms. There was one old ruffian, a designer by trade, a misogynist and foul-mouthed drunk of the worst type. Whenever we met in a tavern in the evening a drinking bout ensued. We would start by conversing and joking, then a bottle of red wine was broached and little by little drinking took pride of place, the conversation would die down and we sat opposite each other in silence, each puffing at his Brissago cigar and drinking his own bottles. We were equals; we both had our glasses filled at the same time and regarded the other with feelings of malice mingled with respect. At grape-harvest time in the late autumn we once went through some vine-growing villages in the Markgräflerland, and at the Stag Inn at Kirchen the old villain recounted his lifestory. It seemed weird and wonderful at the time but unfortunately I have completely forgotten it. The only thing I remember is his description of a drinking episode that took place in his later years. It was the occasion of a village festivity somewhere in the country. As a guest at the table of honour he had even induced the pastor and the village mayor to start their drinking early on in the proceedings. The trouble was that the pastor had to make a speech. After they had managed to drag him onto the platform, he made some outrageous statements and had to be bundled off in disgrace. The mayor stepped into the breach but he put so much vehemence into his extempore discourse that he suddenly felt sick and had to end in an extremely unconventional and indecorous manner.

Later on I could have listened to the old rogue telling me this and similar stories again with great pleasure, but as a result of a quarrel on the evening after a shooting fête we had become irreconcilable enemies, exchanged insults and parted in anger. From then onwards if we happened to be in a tavern together we would sit at separate tables, but from force of habit stared at each other in silence, drank at the same rate and continued to sit there until we were the last customers and were finally requested to leave. But we never got as far as a reconciliation.

My perpetual searchings into the causes of my melancholy and inability to cope with life were fruitless and wearying. Yet I had no sense of being worn out or exhausted; indeed I was conscious of vague stirrings within me, convinced that when my time came I would succeed in producing some valuable work and at any rate snatching a modicum of good fortune from this frail life of ours. But would the right moment ever come ? With some bitterness I thought of those neurotic, up-to-date gentlemen who, with the help of various artificial stimuli, manage to extract some artistic creation from themselves, whereas I was conscious that latent sources of power lay dormant in me, still untapped. And I again examined myself to see what sort of obstacle or daimon was causing my spirit to stagnate and to increasingly weigh me down. I was obsessed with the idea of myself as an outsider, an imperfectly developed human-being whose suffering no one knew, understood or shared. The devilish thing about hypochondria is that it not only makes one ill, but conceited and short-sighted, almost to the point of arrogance. One regards oneself as a kind of dramatic character, little Heine's Atlas, bearing all the world's sorrows and enigmas on one's shoulders, as if there were not thousands of others suffering the same woes, as they wandered about lost in the same labyrinths. Furthermore in my exile and isolation, the fact that the majority of my quirks and qualities were not so much my own as family tra. Camenzind diseases quite escaped my notice.

Every few weeks I went to the professor's house where i gradually got to know all the *habitués* quite well. They were mostly younger university dons, including a number of Germans from all Faculties, besides a number of painters, musicians and a sprinkling of well-to-do citizens, their wives and daughters. I often stared in amazement at these people who acknowledged me with a nod as an occasional visitor. I knew that they saw much of one another, week in and week out. What did they find to talk about all the time? Most of them belonged to the same type of conventional *homo socialis* and they all gave me the impression of being vaguely related to each other because of a gregarious and levelling spirit which was lacking in me. Among them were so many sensitive and striking individuals who evidently lost little or nothing of their freshness and personality by this everlasting sociability. I enjoyed long and interesting conversations with some of them. But what I found intolerable was having to move from one person to the next after a couple of minutes' chat, to lavish compliments on the women, to try to divide my attention simultaneously between a cup of tea, a two-fold conversation, and a piano solo. I hated this discussion of literature and art and I realized that very little real thought was given them, and that most of what was said was insincere. Thus I joined in the game, but my heart was not in it and all this futile chit-chat seemed to me tedious and undignified. I much preferred to hear a mother talk about her children or even to talk about journeys, trivial everyday events and other happenings myself. On such occasions I could become quite friendly and feel thoroughly at home. For the most part, however, at the conclusion of these evenings, I took refuge at an inn where I slaked my parched throat and washed away the unspeakable boredom with draughts of Veltliner wine.

At one of these social evenings I saw my dark girl again. There was a great crowd present, music was played and the chattering was as loud as ever. I sat in a corner, looking folio of sketches of Tuscany. They were not ackneyed views but more intimate sketches of m a personal angle – mostly gifts from travel- s and my host's friends. I had just come across cottage with narrow windows, in the lonely lemente, which I recognized from the many .... stay I had there. The valley is quite close to Fiesole but its lack of antiquities enables it to escape the vast hordes of sightseers. It is a valley of severe yet remarkable beauty – arid, thinly populated, hemmed in between high, bleak mountains; remote, melancholy, and rarely visited.

The girl came up to me and peered over my shoulder.

'Why do you always sit so much apart, Herr Camenzind?'

I was irritated. She is feeling neglected by the other men and now comes over to me.

'Well, no answer?'

'Forgive me, but what reply can I give? I sit on my own because I find it amusing.'

'I am disturbing you then?'

'You're an odd person!'

'Thank you; the feeling's mutual.'

And she sat down. I kept the sheet obstinately in my hand.

'You are from the Oberland, I believe,' she said, 'I'd love to hear you talk about it. My brother says there's only one name in your village – Camenzind. Is that true?'

'Pretty well,' I snapped. 'There is however a baker called Füssli and an innkeeper called Nydegger.'

'Otherwise just Camenzind! And are they all related?'

'More or less.'

I handed the sketch to her. She held the sheet of paper firmly and I noticed that she knew how to look at it and I remarked upon this.

'You're praising me,' she laughed, 'but rather in the way of a schoolmaster.'

'Do you want to look at it any longer?' I asked roughly, 'or can I put it back?'

'Where is it supposed to be?'

'San Clemente.'

'Where's that?'

'Near Fiesole.'

'Have you been there?'

'Yes, several times.'

'What does the valley look like? This only shows a section of it.'

I reflected a moment. The solemn, rugged beauty of the landscape rose before my eyes which I half-closed to try to retain the image. A little time passed before I spoke again, and I was grateful to her for waiting in silence. She realized that I was thinking. I then described San Clemente, how it lay silent, scorched and beautiful in the heat of a summer afternoon. I mentioned that close by in Fiesole various crafts were plied; strawhats and baskets were woven, souvenirs and oranges were sold, tourists cheated or begged for alms. Further down the valley was Florence which enclosed a tide of old and new memories. But neither can be seen from San Clemente. No painters have worked there, there are no Roman remains. History forgot this poor valley. But there the sun and rain battle with earth; there twisted pine-trees struggle for existence, and lean cypresses feel the air with their long slender branches for a hint of an approaching hostile storm which will shorten the bleak lives to which their arid roots cling. Occasionally, an ox-cart goes by from a neighbouring farm or a peasant family passes by on a pilgrimage to Fiesole. But these are only chance visitors, and the red skirts of the peasant women which elsewhere look so gay and lively strike a disturbing note here, and one is not sorry to lose sight of them.

And I told her about my journeys there with a friend when I was a young man and how I had lain at the foot of the cypresses and rested against their lean trunks; and I told her that the lonely and melancholy beauty of that strange valley reminded me of the mountain gorges of my native land.

For a while we remained silent.

'You are a poet,' she said.

I pulled a wry face.

' I don't mean like that,' she went on. 'Not just because you write stories and so on, but because you understand and love nature. What does it matter to other people whether a tree rustles or a mountain glows in the sunshine? For you there is a life in them which you are able to share.'

I replied that no one understood nature and that despite all one's groping and desire to understand, one was merely confronted with enigmas and became depressed. A tree in the sunshine, a weathered stone, an animal, a mountain – all have a life of their own, a history; they live, suffer, defy, enjoy, die, but all this seems beyond our power to grasp.

As I talked, flattered by her quiet, patient attention, I began to look at her. She turned towards me and fixed her steady gaze on my face. Her expression was calm, rapt, and tense with interest. She was listening to me as a child might, or, like a grown-up when listening he becomes absorbed and his eyes unconsciously recapture a child's sense of wonder. And as I looked at her I gradually realized with all the simple joy of discovery that she was very beautiful.

When I stopped talking, she too remained silent. Then she started up dazzled by the lamplight.

'What is your name,' I asked without thinking much about it.

'Elizabeth.'

She went away and was soon afterwards requested to play the piano. She played well. But as I moved up towards her, I noticed that she seemed to have lost some of her beauty.

When I descended the comfortable, old-fashioned staircase on my way home, I caught a few words of a conversation between two painters as they were putting on their overcoats in the hall.

'He spent the whole evening dancing attendance on pretty Lisbeth,' one of them said laughing.

'Still waters . . . ,' replied the other. 'He hasn't made a bad choice either!'

So it had already become the talk of idiots like those. It

suddenly occurred to me that, almost against my will I had confided my most personal memories and a whole period of my most intimate life to this unknown girl. How had I come to do so ? And now malicious tongues were already wagging! Swine!

I went away and gave the house a wide berth for months. As it happened it was one of the two artists in question who first tackled me about it in the street.

'Why don't you go there any more ?'

'Because I can't stand the damned gossip they talk there!' I said.

'Ah yes, our female friends!' he laughed.

'No,' I retorted, 'It's the men I have in mind, and artists in particular!'

I saw Elizabeth during the next months on a few rare occasions in the street, once looking in a shop, and once in the Art Gallery. Normally she looked attractive rather than beautiful. There was something about the movement of her slender body which set her apart and lent her distinction and grace, but occasionally gave her an exaggerated and artificial look. But she was truly beautiful in the gallery. She did not notice me. I was sitting on one side, turning over the pages of the catalogue and she was standing nearby, completely absorbed in front of a large Segantini. The picture represented a group of peasant girls working in some rather poor-looking meadows with rugged mountains in the background – not unlike those of the Stockhorn range, and, above it all, an indescribable, superbly painted ivory cloud in a light, cool sky. Its strangely conglomerate and compact mass struck one immediately. One could see it had just been rolled up and kneaded by the wind and was ready for its slow ascent into the sky. Elizabeth evidently appreciated this cloud, for she was completely absorbed by it. And again her normally withdrawn spirit shone out in her expression, laughed gently in her wide-open eyes, softened her smallish mouth and smoothed away the severe furrow on her forehead, the result of much thought. The beauty and sincerity of a great work of

6

art had overwhelmed a spirit, itself beautiful and sincere; so much was apparent in her face.

I sat quietly close by, contemplated the lovely Segantini cloud and the lovely girl who was under its spell. Then I got into a panic in case she should turn round, see and speak to me and lose her beauty in doing so. Quickly and silently I left the gallery.

It was about that time that I regained my delight in silent nature and that my attitude towards it began to change. I continually sallied forth into the marvellous surroundings of the town, for preference in the Jura. I continually saw the forests and mountains, meadows, orchards and bushes standing as if they were waiting for something. I felt that perhaps it was for me; it was certainly for affection of some kind. And so my love for all these things took shape; a strong, insatiable longing in me rose for their silent beauty. A deep love and longing stirred within me, striving for conscious expression, for understanding and love.

Plenty of people say they 'love nature'. They mean that sometimes they are not averse to allowing its proffered charms to delight them. They go out and enjoy the beauty of the earth, trample down the meadows and gather bunches of flowers, sprays of foliage, only to throw them down or see them wilt at home. That is how they love nature. They remember this love on Sundays when the weather is fine and are then carried away by their own sentiment. And this is generous of them for is not 'Man the crowning glory of Nature'. Alas, yes, 'the crown!'

And so more enthusiastically than ever I explored the basic things of life. I heard the wind sighing in the tree-tops, mountain-torrents roaring down the gorges and quiet streams purling across the plains, and I knew that God was speaking in these sounds and that to gain an understanding of that mysterious tongue with its primitive beauty would be to regain Paradise. There was little of it in books; the Bible alone contains the wonderful expression of the 'groaning and travailing of creation'. Yet I knew deep down inside me that at all times men, similarly overcome by things beyond their comprehension, had abandoned their daily work and gone forth in search of tranquility so to listen to the hum of creation, contemplate the movements of the clouds, and anchorites, penitents and saints alike, filled with restless longing, stretch out their arms towards the Eternal.

Have you ever been in the Camposanto in Pisa? The walls are painted with the faded frescoes of past centuries, one of which depicts the life of the Desert hermits. Even today, despite the faded colour, this naive depiction glows with the magic of blissful peace so that with a sudden pang one longs to confess one's sins and wickedness in some remote place and never return. Countless artists have endeavoured to express their longing in sacred paintings, and any one of Ludwig Richter's tender depictions of children tells the same tale as the Pisa frescoes. Why, for example, did Titian, that lover of the concrete and the tangible, provide his clear, objective paintings with that background of tenderest blue? It merely consists of a strip of warm, deep blue. You cannot see whether it is meant to suggest distant mountains or the boundless horizon. The realist Titian was not aware of this. He did not paint his picture as the art historians like to assert, on a basis of colour harmony alone – it was merely his tribute to the restless, unappeasable element that lurked hidden even in the soul of this happy man who was so much fortune's darling. Art it seemed to me, has always been at great pains to find expression for true innate longing of the divine element in us.

St Francis expressed it in a more mature, yet more childlike way. Now, for the first time in my life I understood him. By his inclusion of the whole earth, plants, animals, the heavenly bodies, winds and water in his love for God, he anticipated the Middle Ages, even Dante himself, and discovered a language to express the eternally human. He deemed all powers and natural phenomena his 'dear brothers and sisters'. When in his later years the doctors condemned him to let them sear his forehead with a red-hot iron, even in the middle of his dread of the agonizing torture he was able to greet his 'dear brother, fire' in this fearful iron.

As this personal love of nature began to grow in me and I listened to her voice as to a friend and travelling companion who speaks in a foreign language, my melancholy, though not cured, was ennobled and cleansed. My ear and eye became more acute, I learned to grasp subtleties and fine distinctions, and longed to hear the pulsation of life in all its manifestations more clearly and at close quarters – perhaps even to understand and enjoy the gift of expressing it in poetic form so that others also could get closer to it and seek out the springs of all refreshment, purification and childish innocence with deeper understanding. For the time being it remained a wish, a dream. I did not know whether it could ever be fulfilled, and I did what was nearest by loving everything visible and by no longer treating anything surrounding me with scorn or indifference.

I find it impossible to describe the restorative and comforting effect this had on my darkened life. There is nothing nobler and more blessed than a quiet, steady, dispassionate love and there is nothing I could desire more than to know that a few, perhaps two, or even only one of those who read these words, were to learn this pure and blessed art through my example. This love is inherent in many and they become unconscious exponents of it throughout their lives; they are the favoured ones of God, the good and the children among men. Many have learned it through some deep sorrow – have you never noticed such people with quiet, thoughtful, shining eyes among cripples and invalids? If you feel disinclined to listen to my poor words, go to those who are changed and illuminated by overcoming afflictions through undemanding love. Even today I am still woefully far from this perfection which I have discovered in many an invalid. Yet throughout these years I have rarely been denied the comfort of knowing how to find the right path to such a feeling. That is not to say that I have always followed it; rather I have delayed at every stopping place on my way and have been guilty of not a few unhappy detours. Two selfish and strong inclinations fought inside me against genuine love: my fondness for solitude and my addiction to drink. I was unsociable and a drunkard. I did in fact cut down my wine consumption to a large extent, but every few weeks the beguiling god would persuade me to throw myself into his arms. I rarely lay helpless on the road or indulged in other nocturnal frolics however, for wine seems to have an affection for me and only entices me so far – never beyond the stage of allowing our respective souls to commune in a friendly fashion. My conscience troubled me after every drinking bout, but in the end my fondness for wine proved too strong to overcome; it was a legacy from my father that I had fostered with solicitude and piety for years, and with which I had completely identified myself. I had therefore to find an escape and I concluded a half-serious pact between my inclination and my conscience; I included 'my dear brother Wine' in the Saint of Assisi's song of praise.

Chapter Six

My other besetting sin was much worse: the company of my
fellow-men afforded me little pleasure. I lived like a hermit
and was always ready to regard human affairs with scorn and
derision.

At the start of my new life, I did not give the matter much
thought. It seemed right to leave my fellow creatures to themselves and reserve my tenderness, devotion and interest for
the inarticulate life of nature. To begin with this completely
satisfied me. When I was about to go to bed at night, I would
suddenly think of a hillside, the edge of a wood, an isolated
favourite tree which I had not seen for a long time. There it
stood in the wind, slumbering, dreaming perhaps, moaning,
stirring its branches. What did it look like ? And I would leave
the house and go towards it, see an indistinct form loom up
in the darkness. I would survey it with affectionate wonder
and bear its vague image away with me.

You will smile. This love may have been mistaken, but it
was not wasted. But how from that stage was I to find the
path that led to the love for human beings ?

Once you embark on a course, the best things seem to come
of their own accord. The notion of my great poetic work
hovered before me, seeming ever more unattainable. And
when my love of nature enabled me to speak the language of
the woods and the trees as a poet, whom would it benefit ?
Not only nature and the things I loved in it, but all human
beings for whom I acted as guide and bearer of the gospel
of love. But as yet I was uncouth, scornful and lacking in
affection in my attitude towards them. I was aware of this

dichotomy and the need to combat this harsh unfriendliness, and to show my fellow men some sympathy. But it was difficult, for in this respect fate and loneliness had combined to make me hard and recalcitrant. It was not enough for me to make an effort at home and in the tavern, to be less boorish and to give the occasional, friendly nod to people I met in the street. Furthermore, I could not help noticing how deeply I had embittered my relationship with others, for my friendly advances were eyed with coolness and suspicion or interpreted as ironical condescension. The worst of it was that I had avoided the house of my friend the scholar – the only place where I could call for the best part of a year, and I saw that it was imperative for me to knock at his door again and find some way of re-entering social life as lived in Basel.

This was where my despised human weakness came to my rescue. Almost as soon as my thoughts went back to that house I seemed to see Elizabeth, as beautiful as when she had stood before the Segantini cloud, and I suddenly realized what a large part she had played in my longing and my melancholy. And then for the first time in my life I thought seriously of choosing a partner. Up till then I had been so convinced of my utter unsuitability for marriage that I had accepted the idea with caustic irony. After all I was a poet, a wanderer, an alcoholic, a lone wolf. But now I believed I recognized a fate eager to provide me with a bridge to the world of humanity, in the shape of a love match. Everything looked so attractive and assured. I had felt and perceived that Elizabeth was not unwilling and furthermore, that she was a responsive and noble personality. I remembered how I had first come to realizing her beauty in the course of our chat about San Clemente and then again as she stood before the Segantini. But for years I had been collecting a rich, inner treasure-store from art and nature. I would teach her to see the latent beauty in everything. I would so surround her with beauty and truth so that her face and soul would shed its sadness and she would be able to fully realize her potentialities. Strangely enough I was completely unaware of the humorous side of my sudden transformation. I, a recluse and an outsider, had turned overnight into an infatuated young fool, who dreams of married bliss and of setting-up home.

I quickly made my way to the hospitable house, where I was received with friendly reproaches. I called there several times, and after several visits I encountered Elizabeth again. She was unmistakably beautiful. She looked exactly as I had imagined her as my betrothed – beautiful and happy. And for an hour I basked in the beauty of her presence. She gave me an amiable, nay, a warm welcome, and a confident friend-liness that delighted me.

Do you remember the evening on the lake, in the boat, that evening with the Chinese lanterns, the music and my declaration of love, nipped in the bud? It was the sad, yet ridiculous story of calf-love. More ridiculous and sadder still is the story of Peter Camenzind, the grown man in love.

I heard casually that Elizabeth was engaged. I congratu-lated her, was introduced to her fiancé who called for her, and congratulated him too. An amiable smile was fixed on my face the whole evening; it weighed on me like a mask. Later, I made my escape but this time neither to the forest nor the tavern. I sat on my bed, stared at the lamp in a state of numb astonishment until it began to smoke and go out. Finally, I returned to this world. Then, once more, sorrow and despair spread their black wings over me, so that I lay small and weak and broken, and sobbed like a child.

Next morning I packed my rucksack, went to the station and set off for home. I felt a longing to climb the Sennalp-stock, to think back to my childhood and discover whether my father was still alive. We had become strangers. My father was greying and already somewhat bowed and insignificant-looking. He treated me with gentle shyness, asked no ques-tions, wanted to give up his bed to me, and he seemed as much embarrassed as surprised by my visit. He still owned the house but had sold the meadows and the cattle and re-ceived a small annuity. He did odd jobs here and there.

When he left me, I went to the spot where my mother's bed had stood, and all the past flowed by me like a broad, peaceful river. I was no longer a youth and I thought how quickly the years would flash by and I should be a grey, bent little man and lie down to a bitter death. In the shabby, almost unchanged little room where I had once learned Latin and had witnessed my mother's death, these thoughts had a soothing naturalness about them. With gratitude I recalled all the rich experience of my youth, and the poem I had learned in Florence, by Lorenzo de Medici, came into my mind:

> Quant'è bella giovinezza,
> Ma si fugge tuttavia.
> Chi vuol esser lieto sia:
> Di doman non c'è certezza.

And at the same time I was surprised to find myself introducing memories of Italy, history, and the wide kingdom of the mind into this old room in my home.

I gave my father some money. In the evening we went to the inn where everything was as before, the only difference being that now it was I who paid for the wine and that when my father spoke of 'Star' wine and champagne he deferred to me, and that I could now hold more than him. I inquired about the old peasant over whose bald pate I had once poured the wine. He had been a wag and a great one for jokes, but was now long dead, and the grass was beginning to grow over his drollery. I drank Vaud wine, listened to the conversation, yarned a little myself and as I went homeward in the moonlight with my father, and he continued to burble away and gesticulate in his drunkenness, I felt strangely spellbound, as never before. I was surrounded by ghosts from the past – Uncle Konrad, Rösi Girtanner, my mother, Richard and Erminia Aglietti, and I gazed at them as when one looks at a picture-book and as one turns over the pages one is astonished how much more lovely and perfect everything seems than in reality. And I saw how everything had vanished, almost forgotten, yet rose clearly and unmistakably before my eyes: half of my life, that my memory had unwittingly preserved for me.

Only when we arrived home and later on in the night when my father lapsed into silence and fell asleep, did my thoughts return to Elizabeth. It was only yesterday that she had greeted me; I had admired her and had wished her fiancé good luck. An interminable time seemed to have gone since then. But my sorrow awoke and mingled with the tide of revived memories and beat against my selfish and vulnerable heart like the *Föhn* against a shivering, tumble-down Alpine hut. Home was unbearable. I climbed through the low window, walked down the garden to the lake, unloosed the neglected punt and rowed gently out into the faintly illuminated water. The silvery, dusky, silent solemn mountains surrounded me; a full moon hung in the bluish night and the peak of the Schwarzenstock almost reached up to it. It was so still that you could hear the faint roar of the Sennalpstock waterfall. The spirits of my home and my youth brushed me with their pale wings, filled my small boat and entreated me with outstretched hands in painful, incomprehensible gestures.

What had been the meaning of my life? Why had so many joys and sorrows passed over me? Why had I suffered from that thirst for truth and beauty, which still remained unquenched? Why in defiance and tears had I suffered love and torment for those desirable women – I who once more today hung my head in shame and tears for unrequited love? And why had an incomprehensible God smitten me with a burning craving for love when he had ordained for me the life of an unloved recluse?

The water lapped gently against the bows of my boat and trickled in silver drops from my oars; the mountains closed silently in on me; the cool moonlight above the mist of the valleys strayed. And the ghosts of my youth stood silently about me, searching me with their deep-set eyes. I even seemed to descry the lovely Elizabeth among them; she too had loved me and would have been mine if only I had been quicker.

It seemed to me that the best I could do was to sink

silently under the pale lake waters; no one would ever inquire about me. Yet when I noticed that the decrepit old boat was leaking I rowed more rapidly. I suddenly felt chilly and hurried to return home and to bed. There I lay in a state of wide-awake exhaustion and thought over my past life in an effort to discover what was wrong with me, what I needed for a more satisfactory and genuine life and a closer communion with the core of existence.

I knew well enough that love is at the heart of all goodness and joy, and despite my recent deep sorrow concerning Elizabeth, I must start learning to love humanity in deadly earnest. But how and whom was I to love?

It was then that I thought of my father and realized for the first time that I had never loved him as I should have. As a boy I had been a thorn in his flesh; later I had gone away and left him alone even after my mother's death, had often been angry with him and finally had almost completely forgotten him. I could not rid my mind of a picture of him lying alone and abandoned on his death bed, he who had been such a stranger to me and whose affection I had never tried to win, with me standing beside him watching his spirit ebb away.

And so I embarked on the difficult yet rewarding art of learning my lesson from a hoary, shabby inebriate instead of from a beautiful and admired sweetheart. I ceased to give him surly answers, attended to his needs to the best of my capacity, read him stories from the Almanack and chatted to him about wines which were produced and drunk in France and Italy. I felt I could not deprive him of his little bit of work, as he would have been so lost without it. Nor did I succeed in persuading him to drink his quart quietly at home with me in the evenings. We tried it out a few times. I fetched wine and cigars and made every effort to help the old man pass the time. On the fourth or fifth evening he was silent and surly, and finally when I asked him what was wrong, he said, 'I don't believe you'll ever let your father go into a tavern again.'

'Nonsense,' I said. 'You're the father and I am the boy and it's up to you to decide what we do.'

He gave me a searching look, then picked up his cap cheerfully and we strolled off together to the tavern.

It was obvious that my father would not have wished me to prolong my stay, although he did not mention it. Besides, in my divided state of mind I badly needed to be away from home in order to get better. 'What would you say, if I went off again one of these days?' I asked him. He scratched his head, shrugged his hunched shoulders, and gave a sly, tentative laugh. 'As you like.' Before I finally started out I called on a few neighbours and on the monks and asked them to keep an eye on him. Then I took advantage of another fine day to ascend the Sennalpstock. From its broad, rounded summit I looked over the mountains and valleys, and gleaming water and the haze that hung over the distant towns. In my boyhood, I had set out to conquer the lovely, distant world, and now it lay spread out before me again, as beautiful and mysterious as ever and I was ready to go out into it again and once more seek the land of happiness.

For the benefit of my studies I had long since resolved to spend more time in Assisi. I began by going back to Basel where I dealt with matters of urgency, put my belongings together and sent them in advance on to Perugia. I myself went no further than Florence and made a slow comfortable pilgrimage southwards. Down there one has no need of any accomplishments to get on friendly terms with the people; their life is continually on the surface and is so simple, open and unaffected that in an undemanding way one makes a host of friends as one moves from one small town to the next. Once more I felt comfortable and at home, and I resolved that when I returned to Basel I should look for the warm proximity of human relationships, not in society, but among the ordinary people.

In Perugia and Assisi my historical work took on a new lease of life. And as the day-to-day existence there was an additional pleasure, my nature soon began to recover from the purposelessness into which it had fallen and to throw out new bridges to life. My landlady in Assisi, a talkative, god-fearing greengrocer, took a great liking to me on the strength of some conversations we had about Saint Francis and brought me the reputation of being a firm Catholic. Undeserved though this honour was, it brought me the advantage of mixing with the people, since I was considered to be free of the taint of paganism which is otherwise associated with every foreigner. The woman in question was called Annunziata Nardini, was thirty-four years of age, and a generously fulsome widow with excellent manners. On Sundays in her gay, floral-patterned dress she looked like the personification of feast-days, for on those occasions, in addition to her earrings she wore a gold chain on her bosom on which a row of medallions tinkled and glistened. She also carried around a silver-bound prayerbook which she would have found difficult to use, and a handsome black and white rosary on a slender silver chain which she could handle more adroitly. When she sat in the *loggetta* during the interval between two church services and described the sins of absent friends to admiring neighbours, the moving expression of a soul at peace with God could be seen on her round, pious face.

As my name was impossible for the people to pronounce, they just called me Signor Pietro. We used to sit together in the tiny *loggetta* in the lovely, sunny evenings – neighbours, children and cats included – or in the shop among the fruit, baskets of vegetables, seedboxes and suspended smoked sausages, and recounted our experiences to each other, discussed the harvest prospects, smoked cigars or sucked at a slice of melon. I told them about Saint Francis, the story of Portiuncula and the church of the Saint, of Saint Clare and the early Franciscan friars. They listened with solemn faces and asked innumerable questions, sang the Saint's praises and switched over to retailing and disclosing more recent and sensational events, among which stories of robberies and political feuds found particular favour. The cats, children and dogs played and fought all round us. Because I enjoyed it and also to maintain my good name, I ransacked the lives of the saints for edifying and moving episodes, and was glad I had brought Arnold's *Lives of the Patriarchs and other Saintly Persons* among the few books I had with me and I translated his naive anecdotes with slight variations into a demotic Italian. Passers-by stayed and listened for a while, joined in the conversation. And so it came about that the company was often renewed three or four times in the course of an evening. Only Signora Nardini and myself sat there permanently and never missed a session. I had my bottle of red wine beside me and impressed these poor and frugal folk by the superior way I made free with wine. Gradually even the timid girls of the locality gained confidence and took part in the conversation from the doorstep, accepted my little prints and began to believe in my piety since I neither made unsuitable jokes nor appeared to be trying to make up to them. There were some large-eyed, dreamy beauties among them who might have stepped out of Perugino paintings. I was fond of them all and enjoyed their friendly and playful company, but I never fell in love with any of them, for the prettiest were so much alike that their beauty always seemed to me to be of race rather than personal. Often we were joined by Matteo Spinelli, a young man and son of the baker. He was a sly, witty fellow; he could imitate lots of animals, knew all the local scandals and was fairly bursting with every kind of effrontery and practical joke. When I recounted legends of the saints he would listen with exemplary piety and humility, but later in a scene of ingenuously framed malicious questions, comparisons and surmises, he would ridicule the holy fathers to the horror of the greengrocer's widow and the undisguised delight of most of his audience.

I frequently sat alone with Signora Nardini, listened to her edifying talk, and took a malicious pleasure in her human frailties. No vice or foible in her neighbours escaped her vigilance. She assigned them their places in purgatory after a process of careful sifting. But she had taken me to her heart and confided in me the most trivial events and told me frankly and in detail what she thought about them. She asked about every purchase I made, what it cost me, and saw to it that I was not swindled. She allowed me to tell her incidents in the lives of the saints, and, in return, let me into the secrets of fruit and vegetable-buying and her cooking. One evening we were sitting in the tumble-down market hall. To the shrieking delight of the girls and the children I had sung a Swiss song and indulged in some yodelling. They wriggled with ecstasy, imitated the sounds of the foreign language and demonstrated the comic way my Adam's apple rose and fell as I performed my yodelling. Then one of the company started talking about love. The girls giggled, Signora Nardini rolled her eyes and heaved sentimental sighs, and eventually they pestered me to speak of my own amorous adventures. I did not mention Elizabeth but told them about my boating expedition with Signorina Aglietti and my thwarted proposal of love. It seemed strange to be recounting this story of which I had not said a word to anyone except Richard, to this Umbrian company, in front of those narrow, cobbled southern streets and the hill with the golden evening glow above it. I told my story spontaneously, after the manner of the old *novella*, yet my heart was in it, and I was secretly afraid my hearers might laugh and make fun of me.

But when I came to the end, I found all eyes fixed on me sympathetically.

'And such a handsome man!' cried out one of the girls vigorously. 'Such a handsome man and he's had such an unlucky love story!'

Signora Nardini, however, passed her soft, plump hand through my hair, exclaiming, '*poverino!*'

Another girl handed me a large pear and when I asked her to take the first bite, she gazed at me solemnly as she did so. When I wanted to let the others have a bite too, she protested and said, 'No, eat it yourself! I've given it to you because you have told us of your misfortune.'

'But you're sure to fall in love with someone else,' remarked a swarthy vine-grower.

'Never,' I said.

'Are you still in love with that wicked Erminia then?'

'Now I always reserve my love for Saint Francis who has taught me to love all men, you and the people of Perugia and all these children here, and even the man Erminia loves.'

A certain element of complication and danger was introduced into this idyllic existence when I discovered that the good Signora Nardini earnestly desired to keep me there indefinitely and marry me. This trifling affair made me into a cunning diplomat, for it was no easy matter to destroy those dreams without at the same time spoiling our harmonious relations and forfeiting the agreeable friendship that existed between us. And I had to bear in mind my journey home. If it had not been for my dreams about the poetry I was going to write and the threatened exhaustion of my funds, I would have stayed there. Perhaps thus impoverished I might even have married Signora Nardini. Yet what really stopped me was my unhealed sorrow concerning Elizabeth and my longing to see her again.

The plump widow sadly but surprisingly bowed to the inevitable and did not allow me to suffer through her disappointment. When the parting came, I cared perhaps more than she did, I was leaving much more behind than I had ever left in my native village and never had my hand been shaken so warmly by so many people on any previous leave-taking. They piled fruit, wine, sweet liqueurs, bread and a sausage into my carriage and I had the unusual sensation of parting from friends to whom it was not a matter of indifference whether I went or stayed. Signora Annunziata Nardini kissed me on both cheeks and as I went off her eyes were full of tears.

Previously I had believed that one must derive a special joy from unrequited love. I had now experienced how painfully embarrassing such proffered love can be when you cannot return it. And yet I could not help being just a little proud that some woman should love me and want me for her husband.

This piece of vanity on my part was indicative of my partial recovery. I felt sorry for Signora Nardini and yet I would not have been without the episode. And I realized more and more that happiness has little to do with the fulfilment of external wishes and that the sorrows of a young man in love, however painful, do not merit the term tragic. It was indeed a great sorrow for me to have to do without Elizabeth. But my life, freedom, work and way of thought – all these were unimpaired – and though remotely I could continue to love her as before, to my heart's content. These thoughts and still more the simple gaiety of my life in the months spent in Umbria had thoroughly restored me. I had always had an eye for the comic and the droll but I had allowed my ironical spirit to spoil the pleasure it afforded me. Now, little by little, I redeveloped an eye for the humours of life, and I found it easier and increasingly possible to reconcile myself with my fate and not begrudge myself the odd tasty morsel or so in the feast of life.

Indeed, when you travel back home from Italy, it is always like that. You snap your fingers at principles and prejudices, smile indulgently, thrust your hands in your trouser-pockets and see yourself as a shrewd man of the world. You have moved around for a brief while in the comfortable and warm life of the South and you are under the illusion that it will continue like that in your own country. Those were my feelings every time I came back from Italy and more especially on that occasion. When I reached Basel and found the old, inflexible way of life, unchanged and unchangeable, depressed and angry, I gradually left my gaiety behind and came down to earth. But I had gained something from my experiences, and never after this did my small boat sail through clear or troubled water without at least one coloured pennant fluttering its confident defiance.

In other ways too, my views had slowly modified. I felt without any great regret that I was saying goodbye to my youthful years and was heading for that period in life when one learns to regard life itself as a brief stretch of road, and oneself as a wanderer whose journeyings and ultimate disappearance from the scene will not move or preoccupy the world to any great extent. One keeps one's eye fixed on some objective or cherished dream without considering oneself in any way indispensable. One therefore indulges in more idle-

7

ness en route so that one can lose a day's journey without a twinge of conscience, lay down in the grass and whistle a tune and surrender oneself unreservedly to the present. Up till then, although I had never worshipped at the shrine of *Zarathustra*, I had thought of myself as a *Herrenmensch* and had a high opinion of myself and a low one of less gifted people. Now I gradually saw with increasing clarity that frontiers are not defined in that way and that life among the poor and down-trodden is not only just as varied but on the whole warmer and more genuine and representative of humanity than that of the favoured and successful.

I returned to Basel at precisely the right moment to attend the first *soirée* at the house of Elizabeth who had got married during my time away. I was in good health, still fresh and sunburnt from my journey and I had plenty of amusing incidents to tell. The lovely Elizabeth was graciously pleased to single me out for her favoured attention, and all the evening I basked in the good fortune that had spared me the disgrace of making a tardy proposal of marriage. For despite my experience in Italy, I still harboured some slight mistrust of the female sex. I felt that women could not help taking a cruel pleasure in the hopeless torments of the men who fell in love with them. A good example of the kind of distressing and mortifying situation in which one could find oneself is implicit in this anecdote of Kindergarten days which I heard from a five-year-old boy. In the preparatory school he attended, the following extraordinary and symbolic custom prevailed. If a boy was guilty of a particularly reprehensible misdemeanour and had to have his bottom smacked as punishment, six little girls were ordered to hold down the struggling victim in the undignified position prescribed for the chastisement. As the said holding-down was considered a great privilege and pleasure, this cruel ecstasy was reserved for the six best behaved girls – the paragons of virtue of the moment. This amusing childhood episode gave me food for thought and has often crept into my dreams, so that I know at least from that experience how much anyone in such a situation must suffer.

Chapter Seven

I had never had any illusions about my gifts as a writer. I was able to live on the proceeds from my work, put a few savings on one side and also send a contribution to my father now and again. He duly took the money along to the tavern, sang my praises and even planned to do me a service in return. I had once told him that I earned my bread mainly from newspaper articles. He therefore thought of me as a kind of editor or reporter, something like those employed by local papers in the provinces, and on three separate occasions he sent me paternal letters in which he recounted events which seemed important to him and which, he believed, would provide me with 'copy' and money. The first item was a barn fire, the second an accident to two climbers, the last the election of a village mayor. He conveyed this news in grotesque journalese. They afforded me great pleasure as an outward indication of a link between us, since they were the first letters I had had from home for years. I found them refreshing too, as a kind of unconscious criticism of my writing, for every month I was called on to review several books whose publication was far less important and consequential than these happenings in the provinces.

In fact at that very moment two books had just been published by authors whom I remembered as extravagant, romantic youths of my period in Zurich. One of them now lived in Berlin and was in a position to describe the shady goings-on, in cafés and brothels in the capital. The second had built himself a luxurious 'hermitage' in the environs of Munich and – in a style that revealed both contempt and despair – alternated between neurotic self-analysis and spiritualistic promptings. The books were given me to review, and, not unnaturally, I made harmless fun of both of them. My neurotic friend was content to send me a contemptuous letter in a style of princely pomposity. The Berlin author, however, made a newspaper scandal out of it. He claimed that I had failed to understand his serious intention, invoked Zola, and blamed not only me for my unsympathetic criticism but the conceited and pedestrian mentality of the Swiss in general. The author, I may add, had spent the only part of his literary career that one might call reasonably healthy and worthwhile in the town of Zurich. I had never been particularly patriotic but there was too much Berlin slickness about it all for me, and I replied to the malcontent in a long epistle in which I was at no pains to disguise my poor opinion of self-important, big-town moderns.

The quarrel made me feel better and it forced me to reshape my conception of contemporary cultural life. This was a tough and tedious task and the result was not wonderfully inspiring, and my book will suffer little if I omit to discuss it here.

All the same, these considerations compelled me to reflect more urgently about myself and my long-planned life's work. It had been my hope, as you know, to write a work of some length which would bring the grandiose, silent life of nature into a close and affectionate relationship with present-day humanity. I wanted to teach the people to be conscious of the pulse of the earth and take part in the life of the universe; not to forget in the bustle of their petty lives that we are not self-created gods but children belonging to the earth and the cosmic whole. I wanted to remind them that, like the songs of the poets and our dreams, the rivers, oceans, drifting clouds and raging storms are symbols and bearers of our hopes which spread their wings between heaven and earth; whose ultimate goal is the confident certainty of the right of citizenship and immortality of all living creatures. Deep down within him every being is convinced of these rights and that he is a child of God who can sleep without fear in the bosom of eternity. Everything that is bad, the diseased, decadent element that we carry round with us, denies such thoughts and believes in death.

But I was also eager to teach men to look for springs of joy and rivers of life in a brotherly love of nature. I wanted to preach the art of seeing, walking and enjoying life, of finding happiness in the present; to make it possible for mountains, seas and green islands to convey their message through their mighty and captivating tongues; to open up the view to the infinitely various manifestations of life as they blossomed day by day and overflowed beyond our towns and houses. I wanted to make people feel a sense of shame that we should know more about foreign wars, fashions, gossip, literature and art than about Spring unfolding its vital force outside our towns and the river that flows beneath our bridges and forests, and the lovely meadows traversed by our railways. I was eager to tell others of the golden chains of unforgettable enjoyment I, a lonely and melancholy person, had found in this world, and I wanted you who are perhaps happier and more cheerful, to discover this world for yourselves with yet a deeper enjoyment. Above all, I wanted to plant the blessed secret of love in your hearts. I hoped to teach you to be true brothers to every living creature and so abound in affection that you no longer need fear sorrow or even death, welcoming it when the time comes as a solemn brother or sister.

All this I did not want to present in the form of hymns and pretentious songs but simply, truthfully, unadorned, with the same mixture of seriousness and humour with which the traveller on his return recounts his experiences of the outside world to his friends.

I wanted, wished, hoped; I know it sounds comic as I say it, indeed I was still waiting for the day on which my vague intentions would assume some sort of order and outline. At any rate I had collected a good deal of material. Not just in my brain, but in the many small notebooks which I carried round with me in my pocket on long and short journeys, one of which I completed every few weeks. In them I wrote down brief observations on the visible life of the exterior world, objectively and without reflection. They were like an artist's notations and I was content to put down things seen in a few words – thumb-nail sketches as it were – of back-streets and roads, descriptions of mountains seen on the sky-line, towns, scraps of conversation overheard between peasants, artisans, market women, doggerel sayings about the weather, notes on light-effects, rain, winds, rocks, plants, animals, bird-flights, wave-formation, colours of the sea, cloud shapes. Occasionally I constructed short stories round them in the form of travel and nature studies which I published; but always without reference to the human element. I had found the story of a tree, animal or the passage of a cloud interesting enough without accessories.

I had often thought that a work of some scope which omitted all allusion to human beings would be nonsense, and yet I clung to this ideal for years and cherished a vague hope that some time perhaps a great inspiration might accomplish what seemed impossible. But at length I realized that I must populate my landscape with human beings and that I would have to represent them as naturally and as faithfully as possible. So I had a great deal of ground to catch up, and this task keeps me busy even today. Previously I had considered human beings only in the mass and had found them fundamentally alien. Since then, however, I have learned how rewarding it is to know and to study individuals rather than humanity in the abstract, and I have filled my notebooks and memory with an entirely fresh set of pictures.

To start with, I found this study quite congenial. I abandoned my naive indifference and became interested in many kinds of people, and saw to what extent the self-evident had eluded me. But I also saw how much travel and observation had opened my eyes and shaped my vision of things. And in accordance with an innate inclination, I was drawn to the company of children which I enjoyed and sought out whenever possible.

Before, I had gained more pleasure from my observation

of cloud and wave than from the study of man. I was amazed to discover that what above all differentiates man from the rest of nature is a kind of protective coat of lies. I soon noted this same trait in all my acquaintances – the result of the fact that every person feels it incumbent upon him to cut a well-defined figure, whereas the truth is that no one knows his true, inmost self. It was with some misgiving that I observed the same trait in myself and I now gave up the attempt to probe the heart of people. The outer jelly in most of them was more important. I found it everywhere, even in children who continually, whether consciously or unconsciously would rather act a part than show their unveiled and natural selves.

After a time it seemed to me that I was making no progress in my task and was getting lost in trivial details. I began by looking for faults in myself but soon I could not disguise the fact that I was disappointed and that the circles in which I moved did not provide the people I was looking for. It was types rather than personalities that I was after and these were not to be found either in academic circles nor among the social set. Longingly I thought of Italy and the few friends and companions of my many rambles there – the ordinary artisans. I had journeyed a good deal in their company and had found many fine fellows among them.

I gained nothing from my visits to local inns and doss-houses. The crowd of casual tramps were no use to me. Thus for a time I was at a loss as to what to do; so I stuck to the company of children and confined my studies to the taverns, where of course there was nothing to learn. Some depressing weeks ensued for I had lost my self-confidence, felt my hopes and wishes must be comically exaggerated, went aimlessly about in the open air a good deal and sat brooding half the night over my wine.

Once more some piles of books which I would have liked to keep instead of disposing of them to the second-hand dealer had found their way onto my shelves; but I had no more room left in my cupboard. To solve the problem I finally discovered a modest carpenter's shop and asked the carpenter to come to my lodgings and take measurements for a bookcase.

He duly arrived. He was an undersized, slow-moving man with a cautious manner. He measured the space, knelt down on the floor, extended his metre-rule to the ceiling – he smelt faintly of glue – and in a childish, painstaking hand jotted down numerous figures in his notebook. In his absorption, he inadvertently collided with a chair, piled high with books. A few tomes fell down and he bent down to retrieve them. One was a small dictionary of vocational slang. It is a book one finds in paper covers in almost all German lodging-houses; a well-produced and valuable little publication. Seeing the familiar volume, the carpenter shot a curious half-pleased, half-suspicious glance at me.

'What is it ?' I asked.

'Excuse me, but I see a book I also know. Have you really studied it ?'

'I've studied tramps' jargon on the road,' I replied, 'but it's nice to look up an expression now and again.'

'Is that so ?' he exclaimed. 'So you've been on the road yourself then ?'

'Not exactly in the sense you mean. But I've journeyed a great deal and spent many a night in a doss-house.'

In the meantime he had picked up the fallen books and was about to go.

'Where have your travels taken you ?' I asked.

'From here to Coblenz and later down to Geneva. It wasn't too bad either.'

'Have you been in jail a few times ?'

'Only once, in Durlach.'

'You must tell me about it, if you've no objection. What about having a chat over a drink ?'

'I'm not too keen, Sir. But if you'd like to spend an evening with me and put a few questions I wouldn't have any objection; that is, provided that you're not just pulling my leg.'

Some days later when Elizabeth was having a *Soirée*, I stopped in the street to consider whether I wouldn't do better to go to my carpenter's. And I turned on my heels, left my frock-coat at home and called on him. His workshop was already shut and dark. I stumbled through a gloomy hall and a narrow court-yard, climbed up the back stairs and finally found a board with the master's name inscribed on it. Proceeding on my way, I came to a tiny kitchen where a thin woman was preparing the supper, simultaneously having to look after three children who filled the small room with a great deal of noise and activity. The woman, who was not particularly glad to see me, led me into the adjacent room where the carpenter sat in the twilight with his newspaper. He grunted doubtfully, at first taking me for an impatient customer; then he recognized me and shook hands.

As he was surprised and embarrassed, I turned my attention to the children; they fled before me into the kitchen and I followed. The sight of the wife preparing a dish of rice brought back memories of my Umbrian Padrona's kitchen and so I lent a hand with the cooking. In our country the lovely rice is mostly ignorantly boiled into a kind of paste which is both insipid and unappetizingly gluey to eat. In fact this disaster was already taking place before me and I was just able to rescue the meal by quickly grasping the saucepan and ladle and taking over the cooking myself. The wife acquiesced in astonishment and the dish proved a tolerable success. We served it up, lit the lamp and I was duly handed a plateful myself.

During the evening the carpenter's wife engaged me in such detailed conversation on household matters that her husband hardly got a word in, and we had to postpone the story of his adventures on the road. These people soon guessed, moreover, that I was a gentleman only in outward appearance and really a peasant's son and of humble birth. The result was that from this very first evening we were soon on an amiable and easy footing. For just as they sensed an equal in me, I smelt my native atmosphere of ordinary people in this poor household. They had no time for refinements, affectations, reticences of any kind; they found the hard, rough life congenial and much too good, even without the cloak of education and higher things, to need arraying with pretty phrases.

My visits to the carpenter's were made with increasing frequency and in his company I was able to forget all about the intellectual set and my own depression and worries. It was like finding a piece of childhood preserved there for me, enabling me to resume the life which the monks had interrupted when they sent me to college.

Bending over a torn and faded old-fashioned map, the carpenter traced our respective journeys, and we were thrilled by every town gate, every street in which we shared common experiences. We recalled our apprentice escapades and on one occasion even sang several of those evergreen *Straubing* folksongs. We discussed business worries, household matters, children, town affairs, and gradually our roles were unobtrusively reversed, and I became the grateful pupil, he the giver and teacher. I felt with relief that I had exchanged a drawing-room atmosphere for the realities of life.

Among his children a five-year-old girl claimed particular attention because she was delicate and set apart from the others. Her name was Agnes but they called her 'Agi'. She was fair – pale with wasted limbs and large timid eyes, and characterized by a gentle shyness. One Sunday when I was about to take the family off for an expedition, I found Agi ill. Her mother stayed at home with her. The rest of us slowly made our way out of the town. We sat down on a bench behind the church of St Margaret. The children hunted for stones, flowers and beetles, while we men looked at the summer meadows, the Binningen grave-yard and the lovely, blue range of the Jura mountains. The carpenter was tired, depressed and silent, and seemed worried.

'What's the trouble ?' I asked when the children were out of hearing. He gave me a forlorn, melancholy look.

'Haven't you noticed ?' he began. 'Agi is dying, I've known it for a long time. The miracle is that she has lasted as long as she has. She has always had a look of death in her eyes. And now there's no hope.'

I began to comfort him, but soon stopped of my own accord.

'Look,' he said with a sad smile, 'you don't believe that the child will survive either. I'm not a pious man as you know and seldom go to church, but I feel sure that the Almighty has a message for me. She's only a child and she's never been strong, but God knows she has been dearer to me than all the others put together.'

Yodelling and shouting a hundred little questions, the children came running back, pressed round me, and made me identify the flowers and grasses they had collected. Finally they insisted on my telling them stories. I told them stories of flowers and trees, reminding them that all these things had a soul and a guardian angel just like children. Their father listened with them, smiled and from time to time gently voiced his agreement. We watched the mountains turn a deeper blue, heard the evening bells and started back home. An evening glow suffused the meadows, the distant towers of the minster soared small and slender into the air, the summer blue of the sky was transmuted into exquisite greens and golds, the trees cast long shadows. The children had become tired and subdued. They were thinking about the guardian angels of the poppies, pinks and hare-bells while we older ones were thinking of Agi whose soul was ready to take wing and leave our little, timid band behind.

The following two weeks all went well, the little girl's health seemed to improve and she was able to leave her bed for hours at a time, and surrounded by her cool pillows looked prettier and happier than ever. Then, for some nights she was in a high fever; we did not need to talk about it for it was obvious to us that the child could not be with us for more than a few weeks or perhaps a few days. On one occasion only did her father bring himself to express his thoughts. He was in his workshop at the time. I saw him rummaging round in his timber and knew without being told that he was selecting boards for his child's coffin.

'It's got to happen soon,' he said, 'And so I prefer to do this myself after work.'

I sat on one of the carpenter's benches while he worked

at the other one. When the boards were planed smooth, he showed them to me with a kind of pride. It was a good, sound piece of pine, free of knots.

'I'm not going to hammer in any nails. I shall joint the boards neatly so as to make a good, enduring job of it. But that's enough for today, let's go up to my wife.'

The days of blazing, wonderful mid-summer went by, and every day I sat with Agi for an hour or two, talked to her about the lovely meadows and woods outside and held her small, frail hand in my broad one, absorbing, as it were, the dear, innocent shining grace which surrounded her until the end.

Then we stood by her bedside, distressed and frightened, and saw her tiny, emaciated body gather its strength to repel all-powerful death which overcame her quietly and without a struggle. Her mother remained calm and controlled but her father lay on her bed and took a hundred last farewells, stroked her fair hair and fondled his favourite child, now dead.

The short, simple burial service was followed by evenings of constraint when the children wept in their beds; comforting pilgrimages to the churchyard where we planted flowers on the fresh grave; where without uttering a word, we sat on the seat among the cool flower-beds and thought of Agi and gazed with new eyes at the earth in which our darling lay; and at the trees and lawns which grew over it, and at the birds whose cheerful songs rang out unrestrained and gay over the quiet churchyard.

Meantime the working-day took its unrelenting course. Soon the children were singing once more, scrapping among themselves, laughing and clamouring for stories, and all of us unconsciously got used to not seeing Agi and thinking of a lovely little angel in heaven.

All this time I had paid no more visits to the professor's parties and very few to Elizabeth's home. But even on those occasions I felt strangely lost and ill-at-ease in the tepid stream of conversation. Now I called at both places only to find locked doors, since they had all gone off into the country, long before. It was only then that I noticed with surprise that absorbed in my friendship with the carpenter's family and the child's illness, I had neglected the hot season and the holidays. In earlier periods of my life I would have found it impossible to remain in the town during July and August.

I went off for a short walking-tour of the Black forest, the Bergstrasse and the Odenwald. I gained an unusual pleasure en route from sending the Basel carpenter's children post-cards of sights at the various beauty spots and from picturing to myself their enjoyment when I told them and their father about the journey on my return.

In Frankfurt-am-Main I decided to extend my holiday for a few more days. In Aschaffenburg, Nurenburg, Munich and Ulm I brought a new appreciation to the historic master-pieces, and I ended by lingering for a time in Zurich. For all these years I had avoided the town like the plague but now I strolled through the familiar streets, sought out the old inns and gardens again and found myself able to think of the wonderful years of the past without regret. The painter, Erminia Aglietti, was married, and I was given her address. Towards evening I went along, read her husband's name on the door, looked up at the windows and hesitated for a moment. Then the old days sprang to life again and my youthful infatuation was roused from its slumber with a gentle ache. I turned on my heels, rather than spoil the picture I had of my beloved Italian friend with a reunion that would serve no purpose. I continued my stroll, visiting the lake-garden where the artists had celebrated their summernight party, and glanced up at the attic of the little house where I had lived three good, all-too-fleeting years.

Dominating all these recollections, the name of Elizabeth sprang unbidden to my lips. The new love was stronger than its elder sisters. It was also quieter, less exacting, more grateful.

To preserve this happy mood, I took a boat out and rowed with slow, easy strokes over the warm, clear waters. Evening was drawing on, and in the sky hung a single, lovely snow-white cloud. I kept it continuously in sight, nodded to it as I thought of my childhood passion for clouds and of Elizabeth, and also the painted Segantini cloud before which I had seen her standing so rapt and beautiful. My love for her, unsullied by any word of unworthy desire, had never seemed so blessed and purifying as now when, with this cloud before me, I glanced back calmly and gratefully at the best moments of my life and felt my previous chaos and passion now replaced by the yearning of boyhood days – and even this had become more tranquil and more mature.

It had been an old habit of mine to hum or sing to the stroke of the oars. I now sang softly to myself and only while doing so did I realize that I was putting verses to the tune. They struck root in my memory and when I got home I wrote them down to celebrate that marvellous evening on the lake at Zurich.

> As a white cloud
> Is poised high aloft,
> So light, lovely and remote
> Are you, Elizabeth.
>
> The cloud journeys on,
> You scarcely heed it,
> Yet it sails through your dreams
> In the dark night.
>
> It sails along and gleams so purely
> That henceforth and forever
> You will suffer a sweet longing
> For that white cloud.

I found a letter from Assisi waiting for me in Basel. It was from Signora Annunziata Nardini and was full of cheerful news. She had found a second husband. But let me quote you her letter:

'My dear Herr Peter,

Allow your faithful friend the liberty of writing to you. It has pleased God to grant me a great piece of good fortune, and I would like to invite you to our wedding on the 12th October. He is called Menotti – he's not very well off, but very much in love with me and has previously been in the fruit trade. He is handsome but not as handsome as you, Herr Peter. He will sell fruit in the

110

piazza whilst I serve in the shop. Our neighbour's lovely Marietta is also about to marry but only a stonemason from another country.

I have been thinking about you every day and have told lots of people about you. I love you as I love the blessed saints to whom I have set up four candles in your memory. Signor Menotti too will be delighted to see you at the wedding. If he did feel at all disposed to be unfriendly towards you, I would stop him! Unfortunately little Matteo Spinelli has proved to be a bad lot, as I have always suspected. He often stole lemons from me. Now he's been taken off to jail for stealing twelve lire from his father, the baker, and for poisoning the dog that belonged to Giangiacomo, the beggar.

I wish you the blessing of God and Saint Francis. I long to see you.

Your devoted and faithful friend,
Annunziata Nardini

P.S. Our harvest was moderate. The grapes did not do very well; there weren't enough pears but plenty of lemons, only we had to sell them too cheap. A terrible thing has occured in Spello. A youth has murdered his brother with a rake – no one knows why – he must have been jealous of him although he was his own brother.'

Unfortunately I was unable to accept the tempting invitation. I sent them my best wishes and proposed to pay them a visit the following spring. I then went off to my friend the carpenter with a present for his youngsters I had brought from Nurenburg. There I found a great and unexpected change. Away from the table, beside the window, crouched a grotesque, deformed figure in a seat with a tray like a baby's chair. It was Boppi, the carpenter's brother-in-law, a wretched, half-crippled hunchback for whom, after the recent death of his old mother, no home could be found. The carpenter had taken him on for the time being with some reluctance, and the cripple's continual presence hung like a blight over the uneasy household. They had not yet become used to him; the children were frightened, the mother was sympathetic but embarrassed and gloomy, the father obviously put out.

Boppi's impressive head with its broad forehead, strong nose and handsome, suffering mouth, sat on an ugly, double hump without a neck. His eyes were bright and calm though a little nervous, and his remarkably small, dainty hands lay perpetually white and peaceful across the narrow tray of the chair. I, too, felt awkward and annoyed about this pitiable intruder, and at the same time I found it embarrassing to have to listen to the carpenter telling the invalid's brief history while the latter sat close by staring at his hands, since no remarks were addressed to him. He was, it appeared, deformed from birth, but had managed to attend the village school and for some years had been able to make himself useful, to a limited extent, by straw-weaving until he had been partially crippled by repeated attacks of gout. For some years now he had been sitting either in bed or in an invalid chair, propped up with cushions. The carpenter's wife understood that in earlier days he had sung to himself quite a lot but for years she hadn't heard him, and never in the present house. He sat there, gazing into space, while all this was being said. It made me feel terrible and I soon took the opportunity of leaving the house, and gave it a wide berth for several days after.

I had been strong and healthy all my life, had never had a serious illness and I looked on invalids, especially cripples, with sympathy tinged with condescension. And so it did not suit me at all to have my present cheerful and cosy life in this artisan household ruined by the unpleasant burden of this wretched creature's existence. I postponed my second visit from one day to the next and vainly tried to devise a scheme for getting the cripple off our hands. There must, I thought, be a way of finding a place for him in a hospital or home at not too high a cost. On more than one occasion I was about to call on the carpenter to talk it over but I fought shy of broaching the subject without him first mentioning it, and I had a childish horror of meeting the invalid again. A shudder ran through me at the thought of having to see him and shake hands with him.

Thus I let a Sunday go by. The following one, I was already about to set out for the Jura mountains in an early morning train when I suddenly felt overcome with shame at my cowardice, stayed at home and after lunch went along to the carpenter's.

I managed to bring myself to shake hands with Boppi. The carpenter was in a bad mood and proposed a walk. He had had enough, he told me, of this continual worry and I was glad therefore to find him amenable to my suggestion. His wife wanted to stay behind but the cripple begged her to go with us; he could quite well be left on his own. Provided he had a book and a glass of water beside him, they could lock the door and leave him without worrying.

So we who thought ourselves fairly kindly and considerate, locked him in and went off for our walk. And we enjoyed it, joked with the children, basked in the lovely, golden, autumn sunshine. None of us felt ashamed, or any compunction at having left the cripple lying there alone in the house. On the contrary, we were only too glad to be rid of him for a while. We breathed the clear, warm air with a sense of relief, and offered the spectacle of a grateful and respectable family enjoying God's Sunday with understanding and gratitude.

It was not until we came to the frontier and went into a restaurant for a glass of wine and were sitting round the table in the garden that the carpenter raised the subject of Boppi. He complained of his unwelcome guest, sighed over the space he took up and the money he cost and ended with a laugh, 'Well, out here at least we can occasionally enjoy ourselves for an hour without him to disturb us.'

This thoughtless remark conjured up a vision of the wretched cripple, appealing to us in his pain; a person whom we did not love, whom we wanted to be rid of and who at the present moment sat there, sad and lonely, shut in and abandoned in a darkening room. For it occurred to me that it would soon be dusk and he would be unable to light the lamp or move any closer to the window. He would have to lay the book on one side and sit in the dark without anyone to talk to or pass the time with, while we were here drinking wine, laughing and enjoying ourselves. And I remembered how in Assisi I had told my neighbours about Saint Francis and had boasted that he had taught me to consider all men as brothers. What had been the point of my studying the Saint's life and learning his wonderful hymn to love and following in his footsteps on the Umbrian hills, if a poor and helpless creature now lay there suffering when I knew about him and it was in my power to comfort him?

I felt an invisible force lay a hand on my heart, press against it and so fill it with pain and shame that I began to tremble and my resistance gave way. I knew that God had a message for me.

'You, a poet!' he seemed to say. 'You, a disciple of the Umbrian saint. You, a prophet who would teach men to love and be happy! You, the dreamer who would claim to hear my voice in the winds and the waters!'

'You love a home where you are treated with affection,' he said. 'Where you have spent many happy hours. And yet the very same day on which I honour this house as my resting-place you flee from it and think of driving me away! Saint, Prophet and poet that you are!'

It was like being confronted with a clear, faithful mirror and seeing myself in it for what I was, a liar, braggart and coward. It was painful, bitter, distressing and terrible. But whatever it was that snapped inside me, suffered torture, reared up wounded, deserved to be broken and destroyed.

I ran off abruptly, left the wine in the glass and the food on the table and hurried back to the town. In my state of excitement I was tortured by an unreasoning fear that an accident might have taken place. A fire might have broken out, the helpless Boppi could have fallen out of his chair and be lying dead or in agony on the floor. I seemed to see him lying there, imagined myself present and powerless to avoid the silent reproach of the cripple's gaze.

Breathless, I reached town and the house, rushed upstairs. It was only then that I remembered that I was standing in front of a locked door to which I had no key, but my anxiety was allayed. Since before I had reached the kitchen door I could hear someone singing inside. It was a strange moment.

Still out of breath and my heart beating fast, I stood on the dark landing. I made no sound myself and listened to the singing of the cripple imprisoned within. He sang a traditional love song about 'The red and white flower' in a soft, gentle and slightly mournful voice. I knew that he had not sung for a long time, and it moved me to hear him using this quiet hour to be happy in his own way for a brief space. Life is like that – mixing comic incidents with things that are serious and fraught with emotion. I was now conscious both of the humour and mortification of my position. For in my sudden panic I had run two or three miles across fields, only to find myself standing keyless in front of the kitchen door! I had the two alternatives: to go off again or shout my good intentions through locked doors. I stood on the stairs, full of my resolve to comfort the poor fellow, show interest in him and help to while away his tedious hours of waiting, and there singing inside he was obliviously sitting, and would merely be frightened if I drew attention to my presence by calling out or knocking. There was nothing for it but to go off again. I hung about the crowded Sunday streets for an hour, by which time the family had reached home. This time it cost me no effort to go and shake Boppi by the hand. I sat down next to him, started talking and inquiring about his reading. It was an easy step to offer to lend him some books and he was grateful. When I recommended Jeremias Gotthelf*, it turned out that he was familiar with practically all that author's works. But Gottfried Keller was new to him, and I promised to lend him some of his books.

Next day when I brought the books I found an opportunity of being alone with him, as the carpenter's wife was just leaving the house and her husband was in his workshop. I confessed how ashamed I had felt at leaving him to himself on the previous day and added that I would be glad to be allowed to sit with him and be a friend.

* Pen-name of the Swiss author, Albert Bitzuis, whose stories of peasant life – *Wie Uli der Knecht glucklich wird, Elsi, die seltsame Magd* – are minor masterpieces.

The little cripple turned his large head slightly in my direction, looked at me and said, 'Thanks very much.' That was all. But to turn his head had cost him a great effort, worth a dozen embraces from an ordinary person, and he had so bright and childlike a gleam in his eyes that I blushed with shame.

But I still had to face the more difficult task of speaking to the carpenter. I felt that my best course was to make an immediate confession of my fears and shame of the previous day. Unfortunately he did not appear to grasp what I meant but at least he was open-minded about it. That is to say he had no objection to my idea of sharing the cripple as our mutual guest. We would share the trifling costs of his keep and I could go in and out to see him as I wished and regard him as a brother.

Autumn that year remained beautiful, and warm for an unusually long time. So the first thing I did for Boppi was to get him a wheel-chair and take him out every day, mostly in company with the children.

Chapter Eight

I seem to have been fated to receive much more from my life and my friends than I could ever hope to return. This was the case in my relationship with Richard, Elizabeth, Signora Nardini and the carpenter, and now in my riper years, full of self-importance, I found myself the astonished and grateful disciple of a suffering cripple. If ever I should complete and publish the work that I had begun so long ago, it would contain little of value that I had not learned from Boppi. A period of happiness now opened before me on which I was able to draw richly for the rest of my life. I was granted the great privilege of having a clear and deep insight into a noble human spirit over whom illness, solitude, poverty and neglect had passed like so many light and fleeting clouds. All the petty vices which normally embitter and wreck our short and beautiful gift of life – anger, impatience, mistrust, falsehood – all those festering sores that disfigure us had been cauterized in this man through a long process of intense suffering; a man who, neither sage nor angel, but full of understanding and resignation, had learned under the stress of terrible pain and deprivation to accept his handicap free of any sense of shame, and to commit himself to God's care. Once I asked him how he managed to come to terms with his weak, pain-racked body.

'It's very simple,' he laughed, 'I wage a perpetual war with my illness. First I win a battle then I lose one, and so the struggle continues. Sometimes we call a halt and truce, keep a suspicious eye on each other and lie in wait until one of us feels ready to take up the challenge again and war breaks out again.'

Hitherto I had always flattered myself that I had sound judgement and was a good observer. However Boppi in this respect, now became my much respected teacher. As he took a great interest in nature and particularly in animals, I often took him to the Zoological gardens. There we spent delightful hours. Before long, Boppi knew every single animal and as we always took bread and sugar with us, many animals got to know us, and we made all kinds of friends. We had a special affection for a tapir whose one virtue is a personal cleanliness rare in his species. Apart from this we found him proud, unintelligent, hostile, ungrateful and extremely greedy. Other animals, the elephant, deer, chamois, even the surly bison, always showed some kind of gratitude for the lump of sugar as they gazed at us trustfully and gladly allowed us to stroke them. But there was no trace of these reactions with the tapir. As soon as we approached he promptly appeared at his bars, chewed slowly and thoroughly whatever we gave him, and when he saw that we had nothing more for him went off without further ado. This seemed to us a sign of pride and character in the animal, and since he neither begged nor thanked us for whatever he was given but accepted it with condescension as an obvious tribute, we called him the tax-collector. Sometimes we had an argument – since Boppi mostly could not feed the animals himself – as to whether the tapir had had enough or whether he could be given a further tit-bit. We weighed up the matter with a scrupulous objectivity as if we were discussing affairs of state. Once when we had already left the tapir behind, Boppi thought we ought to have given him a further lump of sugar. So we turned back, but meantime the tapir, who had returned to his straw couch, blinked haughtily, but did not come to the grille. 'Please, excuse us, Mr Tax-Collector,' Boppi called out, 'but I think we made a miscalculation about a lump of sugar.' Then we went to the elephant who waddled expectantly to and fro, and waved his warm, flexible trunk in our direction. Boppi himself was able to feed him, and he watched with a childlike delight as the huge creature swung his pliable trunk towards him, took the lump of bread from the palm of his hand and blinked his tiny, merry eyes at us with sly benevolence.

I had the keeper's permission to leave Boppi in the Zoo in his invalid chair when I had not time to stay with him, so that on those occasions he could stay in the sun and watch the animals. He would report to me later on what he had observed. He was particularly impressed to see how courteously the lion treated his mate. As soon as she lay down to rest, he contrived to find somewhere to do his restless pacing up and down so that he neither brushed against nor disturbed her in any way by striding past. What amused Boppi most of all was the otter. He never got tired of watching the agile swimming and acrobatics of this lithe creature, and he revelled in it all as he lay back, almost motionless in his chair, although every movement of his head or his arms cost him an effort.

It was on one of the finest days of that autumn that I told Boppi the story of my two love-affairs. By this time we were on such intimate terms that I no longer felt able to keep these unfortunate and not altogether creditable episodes from him. He listened with serious and sympathetic attention but made no comment. Later on he confessed his longing to set eyes on Elizabeth – the 'white cloud' – just once more, and asked me to bear this in mind if we happened to meet her in the street. As this encounter never seemed to take place and the days were already beginning to get chilly, I called on Elizabeth and asked her to grant the poor cripple this pleasure. She was kind enough to consent to my request, and on the day fixed she allowed me to call for her and accompany her to the Zoo where Boppi was waiting in his invalid chair. When the beautiful, well-dressed woman gave the cripple her hand and bent her head towards him, Boppi looked at her almost tenderly with his good, kind eyes in a face brightened with joy. It would have been difficult to decide which of them at that moment presented a more touching sight or which lay closer to my heart. Elizabeth said a few friendly words to him; the cripple could not take his eyes off her, and I stood by, happy to see if only for a moment, the two human beings I most loved and whom fate divided by so wide a gulf, hand in hand before me. After that, Boppi talked of nothing but Elizabeth the whole afternoon; sang the praises of her beauty, distinction, goodness, clothes, yellow gloves and green shoes, gait and the expression of her eyes, voice and attractive hat, whereas to me the sight of the woman I loved dispensing alms to my dear friend seemed painful and grotesque.

Meantime Boppi had read *Der grüne Heinrich* and *Die Leute von Seldwyla* and had become so steeped in the world of these particular books that we shared a common affection for Sulky Pankraz, Albertus Zwiehan and the self-righteous comb-makers*. For a while I wondered whether to give him some of *Conrad-Ferdinand Meyer*'s works to read but it did not seem likely that he would appreciate the almost Latin pithiness of that closely-knit style. Furthermore, I shrank from opening up the abyss of history to those gay, quiet eyes. Instead, I told him about St Francis and gave him Mörike's tales to read. I was struck by his admission that he could not have fully appreciated the story of the *Schöne Lau*† if he had not so often been by the otters' pool where he had been able to indulge in all kinds of remarkable water-phantasies.

It was very pleasant to fall into the closer intimacy of 'thee' and 'thou' with him. It happened spontaneously and when we noticed it one day, we couldn't help smiling and let it continue.

When the arrival of winter put a stop to our excursions and I found myself sitting once more in the parlour of Boppi's brother-in-law, I discovered that this new friendship entailed a certain sacrifice on my part, for the carpenter was continually disgruntled, moody and taciturn. He was not only irritated by the irksome presence of a useless mouth to feed but even more by my relations with Boppi. Sometimes I would

*The novellen referred to are '*Die drei gerechten Kammmacher* and *Pankraz der Schmoller*' contained in the collection '*Die Leute von Seldwyla*' by Gottfried Keller.

†Heroine of Mörike's '*Historie von der Schöne Lau*'

sit for the whole evening chatting happily with the cripple while our host sat by with his newspaper, fuming inwardly. He even crossed his wife who was usually so extremely patient because she insisted – and about this she was adamant – that Boppi should not be sent somewhere else to board. I made several attempts to pacify him and to suggest alternatives but there was no pleasing him. He then began to turn nasty and to jeer at my friendship with the cripple and to make the latter's life a misery. It must be admitted that the invalid and I, who spent a great deal of the day sitting with him, took up a good deal of room in the small house, but I had not given up hope that the carpenter might, like us, grow fond of the invalid. In the end it became impossible for me to do anything which would not either offend the carpenter or cause awkwardness for Boppi. As I have always hated making rapid and important decisions – even in my Zurich period Richard had nicknamed me Petrus Cunctator – I waited for weeks and continually suffered from the fear of losing the friendship of either or possibly of both of them.

The increasing constraint brought about by this difficult situation resulted in my paying more frequent visits to the tavern. One evening after the whole wretched business had made me particularly angry, I sought refuge in a small Vaudois wine shop and drowned my sorrow in several litres of wine. For the first time in two years it was all I could manage to get home without collapsing in the road. Next day, in a delightfully calm mood – as always after a drinking bout – I plucked up courage, called on the carpenter with the idea of putting an end to the farce once and for all. I suggested that he should commit Boppi entirely to my charge, and he showed himself not disinclined to accept my proposition. Finally after a few days' reflection he gave his full consent.

Soon afterwards, I set up home with my poor cripple in a newly rented dwelling. It was like getting married, for now I had to exchange my usual bachelor quarters for a small, orderly household for two. And it went well, even though I was involved to start with in some unfortunate housekeeping experiments. A daily help saw to the cleaning and washing. We had our food brought to the house, and soon we both found ourselves thoroughly happy and at ease in our life together. From now onwards, the need to give up my carefree walks and excursions had not yet begun to distress me. The close presence of my friend was comforting and conducive to my work. All the little attentions an invalid requires were new to me, and at first not particularly pleasant, especially the dressing and undressing him. But my friend was so patient and grateful that he made me feel ashamed, and I went to considerable pains to look after him properly.

I called very few times on my professor friend, more frequently on Elizabeth whose home, in spite of everything, continued to have a fascination for me. There I would sit, drink tea or a glass of wine, watch her play the hostess, now and again suffering from fits of sentimentality although I never ceased to inwardly jeer at any Werther-like feeling that welled up in me. The soft, youthful egotism of love had left me for good. The relationship between us took the shape of an elaborate but friendly state of mock-hostilities and we rarely met for any length of time without indulging in the most amiable of quarrels. Her mind was lively and in a feminine way rather illogical and so this intelligent, clever woman was not ill-matched with my amorous yet crossgrained ways, and since at heart we had a great respect for each other, we could do battle all the more fiercely over every trifle that arose. It struck me as particularly comic that I should be defending bachelordom against the woman whom a little while before I would have given my eyes to marry. I could even tease her about her husband who was a good fellow and proud of his witty wife.

Underneath, my old love still burned for her, but the old exacting fire was now replaced by a wholesome and permanent glow that keeps the heart young and where a hopeless confirmed bachelor can occasionally warm his hands on winter evenings. And now that I had Boppi continually by me, giving me the assurance of a lasting and open affection, I felt able to allow my love to linger on with impunity as a relic of my youth and the spirit of poetry. Furthermore, Elizabeth's typically feminine provocation helped me to cool off and feel grateful for my bachelor state.

Ever since Boppi had shared my quarters I had begun to neglect Elizabeth's house more and more. I spent my time with Boppi, reading books, turning over pages of travel albums and diaries, and playing dominoes. We also livened things up by acquiring a poodle, saw the beginning of winter from the window and every day indulged in endless witty, as well as nonsensical duologues. The invalid had gained a breadth of vision, a practical, good-humoured view of life from which I daily learned something.

When heavy snowfalls occurred and winter displayed its unsullied beauty at our windows we huddled by the fire and gave ourselves up with boyish ecstasy to this indoor idyll. It was then that I learned the art of understanding people which previously I had almost stood on my head to acquire to no purpose. A quiet, yet acute observer, Boppi could conjure up endless pictures from the experience of his earlier surroundings, and once he launched out, he could tell a wonderful story. Although he had hardly known more than three dozen people in his life and had never joined in the great throng, he knew more of life than I did, for he made a habit of observing the tiniest detail and finding a treasure of experience, joy and understanding in every person he met.

The animal world continued to be our favourite source of amusement. We wove stories and fables of every sort round the creatures in the zoo which we could no longer visit. We did not tell them as narratives but concocted them spontaneously in dialogue form; it might be a declaration of love between two parrots, family quarrels between bisons, an evening *causerie* between wild boars.

'How are you, Herr Marten?'

'Only so so, thanks, Herr Renard. You will remember that when I was caught I lost my dear wife. She was called Bushy-tail, as I've already had the honour to inform you. A gem of a woman, I assure you, a . . .'

'Oh, quit your old stories, neighbour. You've told me so often about that gem of yours, if I'm not mistaken. Heavens above, we only live once and we oughtn't to spoil the little pleasure we have . . .'

'Excuse me, Herr Renard, but if you had known my wife, you would be in a better position to understand.'

'Yes, surely. She was called Bushy-tail, wasn't she ? An extremely attractive name – something to caress! But as I was going to say – have you noticed how the sparrow menace is on the increase again ? I have therefore evolved a little plan.'

'To do with the sparrows ?'

'Yes . . . sparrows. Look here, this is my idea. We will put some food in front of the bars, squat down quietly and wait for the little beggars. I'd be surprised if we didn't catch one of them that way.'

'Excellent, neighbour.'

'Would you be good enough then to put some crumbs down. Good! But perhaps you should push them over to the right a little more; that'll be better for both of us. Unfortunately I've no bread to spare at the moment. Good! Look out. We'll lie doggo now and close our eyes for a bit – but hush, here's one flying down now!' Pause.

'Well, Herr Renard, nothing so far ?'

'How impatient you are! As if you'd never been hunting before! A hunter must learn to wait, wait and wait again. So, once more!'

'But where's the bread gone, then ?'

'I beg your pardon ?'

'The bread's gone!'

'Impossible! The bread ? Indeed it's vanished! Well, I'm blowed – that cursed wind again!'

'I have my own ideas about that. I thought I heard the sound of munching a moment ago.'

'Me ? Eating ? What could I have eaten ?'

'The bread, presumably.'

124

'You're offensively pointed in your insinuations, Herr Marten. One can take a remark from a neighbour I should hope, but that's going too far! I repeat, too far! Do you understand? So, I'm supposed to have stolen the bread, is that it? What was it all about? First I was to listen to the feeble tale of your gem of a wife for the thousandth time, then I had a brain-wave that we should put out some bread . . .'

'But that was me! I produced the bread.'

. . . 'Put out some bread; I lay down and watched, everything goes according to plan; then you start gassing away as usual – the sparrows naturally have been and gone, the hunt is ruined and now to top it all I'm supposed to have eaten the bread myself! Well, you can wait here and whistle before I have anything more to do with you . . .'

Thus our afternoons and evenings went swiftly by. I was in the best of spirits, despatched my work with speed and zest, and could hardly believe I had been so lazy, ill-tempered and depressed before. Even the best times with Richard could not match these quiet, cheerful days when the snowflakes danced outside and we sat cosily with the poodle by the fireside.

And then my beloved Boppi had to go and commit his first and last piece of foolishness. In my contented state I had naturally enough been blind to the fact that he was suffering more pain than usual. He, however, with his sheer goodness and affection, assumed a more cheerful air than ever, never uttered a complaint, nor even asked me not to smoke. Meantime he lay there at night in pain, coughing and moaning gently. Quite by chance when I was working late into the night in the room next to his and he imagined I had gone to bed long ago, I heard him groan. The poor chap was startled and taken aback when I suddenly entered his room, holding a lamp. I put it down, sat on the edge of the bed and questioned him. He tried to evade the issue for a time but in the end the truth came out.

'It's not as bad as all that,' he said modestly. 'Just a cramped sensation round the heart when I move a lot and often when I breathe.'

125

He was apologetic about it as if his illness was a crime.

Next morning I consulted a doctor. It was a beautiful, clear day and my depression and anxiety left me as I went on my way. I thought about Christmas and what I could get to please Boppi. The doctor was still at home and in response to my urgent request, came immediately. We set off in his comfortable carriage, went upstairs, entered Boppi's room and then followed the sounding and ausculation, and as the doctor became a little more serious and his voice a trifle more sympathetic, all my optimism oozed out of me.

Gout, weakness of the heart – serious case – I listened and made notes and was surprised to find myself making no objection when the doctor said the patient must be transferred to hospital.

The ambulance arrived during the afternoon, and when I came back from the hospital, I felt terribly alone in the house. The poodle pressed himself against me, the invalid chair was moved to one side, and the room next to me was empty.

That is how it is with the ties of affection. They bring sorrows in their train, and I have suffered a great deal from them in subsequent years. But then it is of so little account whether you have many sorrows to bear or none, as long as one can live with and for others and one is aware of the bond that binds all living creatures together, provided above all that you do not allow affection to diminish. I would give all the happy days I have ever enjoyed and all my love affairs if only I could re-experience the deep insight into those sacred things granted to me during that period of my life. It is a bitter sorrow for eyes and heart; pride and self-esteem have hard knocks to take, but later on one feels so calm and unexacting, so much wiser and so much alive, in one's innermost being.

Already a piece of my old self had perished with the fair-haired Agi. Now I had to see my hunchback friend to whom I had devoted all my affection and with whom I had shared my life, suffer and slowly die day by day, nor did I escape a part in all the terror and sanctity of death. I was still an apprentice in the art of loving and was to embark now on the difficult chapter of the art of dying. I am not going to draw a veil over this period as I did over my Paris years. I prefer to talk unrestrainedly about it, as a bride might about her wedding or an old man about his youth. I witnessed the death of a person whose life had consisted of nothing but love and pain. I heard him joke like a child while he could already feel death at work within him. I saw how his eyes sought mine from the depth of his suffering; not to ask for pity but to console me and show that these spasms and torments had left the best part of him intact. During those moments the pupils of his eyes dilated and I no longer saw his drawn face, but only his bright expression.

'Can't I do anything for you, Boppi?'

'Talk to me about something. Perhaps about the tapir.'

So I talked about the tapir. He closed his eyes and I had a struggle to speak in the old way, for I was very near to tears. And when I thought he was no longer listening or had fallen asleep, I immediately stopped. Then he would open his eyes again.

'And then . . .?'

And I went on telling him about the tapir, the poodle, my father, the bad little Matteo Spinelli, Elizabeth.

'Yes, she's married a stupid fellow. That's the way of the world Peter!'

He would often start discussing the subject of death.

'It's no joke, Peter. The toughest job is nothing compared with dying. But one manages it somehow.'

Or: 'Once the pain is gone, I can laugh again. Death will do me the service of ridding me of a hump, a short foot and a deformed hip. It will be a pity when your turn comes – you with your broad shoulders and fine, strong legs.'

And on one occasion towards the end, he woke up out of a short sleep and said quite loudly. 'There's no such thing as the heaven described by the parson. Heaven is something much better, much better.'

The carpenter's wife often came along and helped in an

understanding and sensible way. To my great sorrow, however, the carpenter himself never turned up.

'What do you think?' I asked Boppi, 'will there be a tapir
in heaven too?'

'Oh, yes.' And he nodded. 'Every species will be represented, even chamois!'

Christmas came and we had a small celebration by his bedside. There was a hard frost, then it thawed again followed
by a fall of snow on the smooth ice. But I did not really notice
all this. I heard and immediately forgot that Elizabeth had
given birth to a son. A comic letter came from Signora Nardini
which I hastily read through and put on one side. I hurried
through my work, continually conscious of stealing every
hour I could, to spend with the invalid. Then, restless and
impatient, I dashed into the hospital where I found an atmosphere of serene calm and I sat for hours at a time by Boppi's
bed, with a deep, dream-like peace around me.

Shortly before the end, he enjoyed some better days. The
extraordinary thing was how the time that had just gone by
seemed obliterated from his memory and he was now entirely
re-living his early years. For two days he spoke only of his
mother. He could not talk for long at a time, but it was obvious
in the hour-long intervals that she was still very much in his
mind.

'I've told you far too little about her,' he said sadly. 'You
must not forget what I tell you about her or there'll be no one
else to know about her and be grateful to her. It would be a
wonderful thing, Peter, if everybody had such a mother. She
never packed me off to the almshouse when I could not work
any more.'

He lay there, breathing with difficulty. An hour passed and
he began talking again.

'She loved me best of all her children and kept me with her
right up to her death. My brothers emigrated and my sister
married the carpenter, but I stayed at home, and, poor though
my mother was, she never allowed me to suffer for it. You
must never forget my mother, Peter. She was a diminutive

128

person, perhaps even smaller than I am. When she gave me her hand it was as if a tiny bird had perched on it. A child's coffin will be large enough for her, that's what neighbour Rütiman said when she died!'

A child's coffin would have accommodated him too. He lay so small and shrunken in his clean, hospital bed, and his hands now looked like those of a sick woman – long, narrow, white and slightly crooked. When he stopped day-dreaming of his mother, my turn came. He spoke about me as if I were not there.

'He's been an unlucky fellow, indeed, but he's none the worse for it. His mother died too soon.'

'Don't you recognize me any longer, Boppi?' I asked.

'Indeed I do, Herr Camenzind,' he said jokingly and gave a gentle laugh.

'If only I could sing,' he added immediately after.

On his last day he asked, 'I say, does it cost a lot in the hospital here? It might get too expensive.'

But he did not seem to expect a reply. A slight blush crept over his pale cheeks, he closed his eyes and for a while looked the picture of a supremely happy man.

'He's sinking,' said the nurse.

But he opened his eyes once again, gave me a roguish look and raised his eyebrows as if trying to signal something to me. I stood up, placed my hand under his left shoulder and gently raised him up, which always made him more comfortable. As he leaned thus against my hand, his mouth was distorted by a short spasm of pain, then he turned his head slightly and shuddered as if he felt a sudden chill run through him. It was the final release.

'Are you all right?' I asked. But he had already left all pain behind and was growing cold beneath my hand. It was one o'clock in the afternoon of the 7th January. Towards evening we carried out the last offices, and the little shrunken body lay peaceful and clean, his face no longer distorted, until the time came for him to be taken away for burial. During the next two days I was continually surprised not to find myself

9

sad and bewildered. I could not even weep. I had felt the separation and the last parting so deeply during his illness that my emotion was dried up, and the dipping scales of my grief slowly lightened and regained their balance.

Nevertheless it now seemed the moment for me to slip away from the town and find somewhere to recover – in the south, if possible – and to stretch as it were the fabric of my work, still only roughed out on the loom. I still had a little money left, so I abandoned my literary commitments and prepared to pack and depart at the first signs of Spring. I should begin by going to Assisi where the vegetable woman was expecting me to visit her, then to as quiet a mountain village as I could find, to do some hard work. I felt that I had now sufficient experience of life and death behind me to warrant my holding forth to others on the subject. With cheerful impatience I waited for the arrival of March. I could already hear characteristic Italian imprecations ringing in my ears in anticipation, and my nostrils were already tickled by spicy smell of risotto, organes and chianti.

I could see no flaw in my plan and the more I considered it, the better it seemed. However, I did well to savour my chianti in advance for things turned out very differently. An odd letter, fantastically phrased, from the innkeeper, Nydegger, announced to me that there had been heavy snow-falls in February and that things in the village, both for cattle and inhabitants, were far from well. My father's situation was particularly critical, and that all in all, it would be a good thing if I could send money or come in person. As it was not convenient to send money and I was really worried about my old father, I felt I must go at once. One grey day I arrived. A blizzard screened mountains and houses from view, and it was a lucky thing for me that I knew the way blindfold. Old Camenzind was not bedridden, as I had expected, but sat miserable and morose by the kitchen range, kept in order by a neighbour who had brought him some milk and was lecturing him about his evil ways and who continued her harangue, not a whit abashed by my arrival.

'Look, here's Peter!' remarked the hoary sinner and winked at me with his left eye.

But she went on with her sermon, undeterred, I sat down on a chair, waiting for her stock of Christian charity to dry up, and I found some remarks in her sermon not altogether inapplicable to me. In the meantime I watched the snow melting from my coat and boots and form first a damp area, then a quiet pool round the legs of my chair. It was not until the woman had talked herself to a standstill, that the official reunion – in which she amiably participated with good grace – was allowed to take place. My father had become much frailer. I recalled my previous short attempt to look after him. It had after all not helped to leave him as I had done, and I should still, since my presence was now more necessary than ever, be reaping the consequences. After all one could not expect a gnarled old peasant, who was hardly a pattern of virtue in his better days, to become sensible in his dotage or to be in any way affected by the spectacle of filial love. Nor was he. In fact, as he grew feebler he became more unpleasant and paid me back all the trouble I had caused him, if not with interest at any rate in full measure. He was sparing and cautious with his remarks but he contrived without the help of words to be bitter, disgruntled and hostile in a number of ways. At times I wondered whether in my old age I should become a similarly irritating and awkward customer. His drinking days were virtually past, and he enjoyed a glass of the 'warm south' which I poured out for him twice a day with ill grace, because I always took the bottle back to the empty cellar and never trusted him with the key.

It was not until the end of February that those bright weeks reappeared which make a miracle of winter in the high Alps. The lofty, snow-covered peaks stood out clearly against the cornflower-blue sky and looked fantastically near in the transparent air. Meadows and slopes were covered with that winter mountain snow, white, crystalline and astringent, which is never to be found in the valleys. At noon the sunshine seems to play particularly round all the little bumps in the snow, deep-blue shadows linger in the hollows and on the slopes, and the air is so purified after weeks of snow-falls that you feel exhilarated with every breath you take. The young people indulge in sledging on the gentler slopes, and in the hour after midday you see the aged standing about in the streets, sunning themselves, while at night the rafters creak in the frost. In the midst of dazzling snow-fields the lake that never freezes lies there blue and calm, lovelier than it can ever look in summer.

Every day before dinner I helped my father to the porch, watched him stretch his brown and gnarled fingers in the beautiful warm sunshine. After a while he would begin to cough and complain of the cold. It was one of his harmless devices for inducing me to give him a drink, for neither cough nor chill were to be taken seriously. In this way he inveigled a small glass of gentian spirit or absinth out of me, stopping his cough after artistically calculated intervals, no doubt chuckling inwardly at having outwitted me. After dinner I left him to himself, strapped on my leggings and went off up the mountains for a few hours, as high up as time allowed. Then I would sit on an old sack I had taken with me, and toboggan back home over the steep snow-fields.

When the time came for my proposed visit to Assisi, the snow lay over three foot deep. There was no Spring until April, bringing with it a villainously rapid thaw such as had not occurred in the village for years. Night and day we could hear the Föhn blowing, the crashing of distant avalanches and the angry roar of the mountain torrents, carrying great boulders of rock and shattered trees along with them and hurling them onto our narrow strips of land and orchard meadows. I could not sleep for what we call the Föhn-fever. Night after night, nerve-racked and anxious, I could hear the moans of the wind, the thunder of the avalanches, the raging waters of the lake beating against the shores. And in the feverish time of that terrible Spring warfare, once again I was attacked by my suppressed love-sickness, so violently that I got up in the night, leaned against the French window and in my bitter frenzy called out words of love to Elizabeth into the tumult of the storm outside. Since that warm night in Zurich when I had raved in this way on the hill overlooking the house of my Italian painter, passion had never made so vicious and irresistible an onslaught on me. I now frequently felt the presence of the beautiful woman quite close to me, seemed to see her smiling and withdrawing at every step I took in her direction. Wherever my idle thoughts strayed, they always returned to the particular image, and like a wounded man, I could not help scratching the itching sore. The shame I felt was as tormenting as it was useless. I cursed the Föhn and in all my torments I was conscious of a similar sensation of silent ecstasy as I had experienced in my boyhood days when my thoughts turned to pretty Rösi and the dark, warm wave of passion swept over me.

I realized that there was no cure for this malady, but at any rate I tried to work for a while. I embarked on the plan of my *magnum opus*, roughed out some ideas but soon saw that the time was not yet ripe. Meantime disquieting reports of damage by the Föhn were coming in on every hand, and in the village itself the emergency dominated the situation. The dams were half destroyed, many houses, barns and stables had suffered heavy damage and several homeless people arrived from outside the parish. Everywhere it was a story of distress and emergency and lack of money. It was during these days that to my joy the major sent for me to call on him at the council chamber, where he asked me if I would be willing to become a member of a relief committee. I should be representing our parish at the Canton and through the medium of the press I was to urge the country as a whole to give help and money. The request was opportune; it provided a chance of sinking my present useless sorrows in a more serious and worthy cause into which I threw myself heart and soul. I wrote to people in Basel and soon found some collectors. The Canton itself, as we knew already, possessed no funds and could only send a few workers. So I turned my attention to the newspapers with reports and appeals; letters, contributions and inquiries poured in and in addition to all the correspondence I had to battle with hard-headed peasants concerning parish council matters.

These few weeks of strenuous unavoidable work did me good. By the time the situation had gradually been mastered and I had become less indispensable, the meadows were becoming green again and the lake was turning its blue, sunny and innocent mirror towards the slopes, now free of snow. My father was having tolerably good days and my infatuation with Elizabeth had vanished like the last sullied snow from the avalanches. It was the time of the year when in the old days my father used to paint his boat, while mother looked on from the garden and I watched him pottering about with the smoke curling up from his pipe, and the yellow butterflies on the wing. But now there was no boat to re-paint, my mother was long dead and my father was maundering round the neglected house. Uncle Konrad also reminded me of the old days. Unobserved by my father, I often took him along to the tavern to have a glass of wine and I would listen to him with good-natured laughter and not a little pride, as he yarned and reminisced about his many hair-brained schemes. He had now given up devising them and the years had left their mark on him. Nevertheless, there was still a certain boyishness and youth in his way of talking and his laughter which it did me good to hear. He proved a source of comfort and amusement on many occasions when I couldn't stand being at home with my father any longer. When I took him along to the inn, he trotted by my side and nervously tried his best to keep his thin bow-legs in step with mine.

'You ought to do some sailing again,' I suggested, to cheer him up, and this talk about sailing invariably led on to the subject of our old boat, no longer in existence, whose loss he lamented as if it had been some well-loved friend. As I too had adored the old wreck and missed it, we revived our memories of all the stories concerning it in great detail.

The lake was as blue as ever, the sun no less bright and warm, and in these later years I often watched the yellow butterflies, with a feeling that there had been little essential change since those days, and that I could quite well go off and lie down in those meadows and indulge in boyish hopes. But it was obvious to me every day now as I washed my face with its prominent nose and melancholy mouth, which smiled back at me from the rusty metal dish, that this was not really so and that I had used up a fair portion of my years. Camenzind senior also saw to it that I should not cherish any illusions about the way times had changed, and if I wanted to be jerked back completely into the present, all I needed to do was to open the tightly-jammed table drawer in my room in which my *magnum opus*, consisting of a packet of faded sketches and six or seven quarto sheets of rough drafts, lay dormant. But I hardly ever opened the drawer.

As well as looking after the old man, I had to repair our tumble-down house which provided me with plenty to do. There were gaping holes in the floor-boards, fireplace and range needed repairing, smoked and stank us out, the doors wouldn't shut properly and the ladder-stairway leading to the loft, once the scene of my father's chastisements of me, was a danger to life and limb. Before anything could be done, the axe had to be ground, the saw set, a hammer borrowed and nails found. The next question was to salvage usable pieces of wood from what was left of the old supply. Uncle Konrad lent me a certain amount of help with the repairing of the tools and whetstone but he had become too old and bent to be of much use. It meant that I had to tear my soft, white fingers to shreds on the stubborn wood, work the ramshackle grindstone-treddle, clamber about on the leaky roof, nail, hammer, tile and chip; in all of which procedures I sweated off some of the weight I had put on. Sometimes, especially when engaged in the arduous task of roof-patching, I would pause in the middle of hammering, sit down, take a pull at my half-extinguished cigar, look into the deep blue of the sky and bask in my idleness with the cheerful certainty that my father could no longer goad me on or find fault with me. If neighbours went past, women and school children, I covered up my inactivity by indulging in friendly exchanges with them, so that I gradually acquired the reputation of the kind of person one could stop and chat with.

'It's warm today, Lisbeth, isn't it?'

'Yes indeed, Peter. What are you doing?'

'Patching the roof.'

'About time too, it's been needing it long enough!'

'True.'

'How's the old chap doing? He must be seventy if he's a day.'

'Eighty, Lisbeth. And to think that we shall be that age some day! No joke is it?'

'You're right there, but I must hurry on now, my husband will want his food. Goodbye for the present.'

And while she continued her journey with the dish swathed in a cloth, I blew clouds of smoke into the air, followed her with my eyes and wondered how it was that everybody else went about their tasks with such energy whereas I had already been hammering away at the same plank for the best part of a couple of days. However, the roof was finally repaired. For once, my father took an interest in all this, and as I couldn't possibly drag him up onto the roof, I had to produce a detailed account of every board I replaced, which gave me an irresistible opportunity for boasting.

'That's all right,' he admitted, 'I would never have believed you could get through it this year.'

When I look back on all my journeys and efforts and reflect on them, I feel both pleased and angry that I have proved as it were the old adage that 'fish belong to the sea and farmers to the land' and that no amount of trying will ever turn a Camenzind from Nimikon into a polished citizen of the town or world. It is a situation to which I am becoming accustomed, and I am glad that my clumsy pursuit of happiness in the world has brought me back, against my will, to the familiar corner between lake and mountains where I belong, and where my virtues and weaknesses, especially the latter, are the normal and traditional ones. In the world out-side I had forgotten my native place and had been very near to considering myself a rare and remarkable plant. Now I see once again that it was merely the spirit of Nimikon that hung about me, unable to adjust itself to the customs of the world at large. Here, however, it does not occur to anyone to think of me as in any way an outsider, and when I look at my old father or Uncle Konrad I feel myself to be a very ordinary son and nephew. My few excursions into the realm of the mind and so-called world of culture can be compared to my uncle's famous sailing episode, except perhaps that they cost me more in money, effort and precious time. Outwardly too, now that my cousin Kuoni has trimmed my beard and I go about again in leather shorts and in my shirt-sleeves, I have turned native once more and when I become old and grey I will take my father's place and humble share in village life, and no one will notice. The inhabitants merely know that I have spent some years abroad, and I take good care not to tell them of the unsavoury existence I led and the number of awkward situations in which I landed myself; otherwise I would soon be the target of their jokes and they would find some derisive nickname for me. Every time I talk of Germany, Italy or Paris, I preen myself a little and sometimes I come to doubt my own veracity even in the more factual parts of my stories.

What then has been the outcome of so many mistakes and wasted years? The woman I loved and still love, is bringing up two attractive children in Basel. The other woman, who loves me, has found consolation and continues her trade in fruit, vegetables and seeds. My father who was the cause of my home-coming, is neither dead nor recovered but sits op-posite me in his iron bedstead, gazes at me and envies my possession of the cellar-keys.

But that is not the whole of the story. Apart from my mother and the drowned friend of my youth, I have the fair-haired Agi and my small crippled Boppi in the world beyond. And I have seen houses in the village patched up again and the river-bed mended. If I so desired, I could also sit on the parish council. But there are plenty of Camenzinds on it already. A new vista has opened up to me lately. The landlord Nydegger in whose parlour my father and I have drunk so many litres of Veltliner, Valais or Vaud wine, is beginning to go downhill rapidly and has ceased to take any further joy in his business. He was telling me his troubles the other day. The worst of it is that if no local person finds the means, an outside brewery will buy up the place and then it will be spoilt, and we shall no longer have a cosy tavern. Some outside tenant will be installed who will naturally prefer serving beer to the wine, and under whose management Nydegger's good cellar will be adulterated and spoilt. I can't stop worrying since this thought has occurred to me; I still have a little capital in the bank at Basel and old Nydegger wouldn't find me an unworthy successor. The only snag is that I could hardly become the landlord in my father's lifetime. For not only would I be unable to keep the old man from drinking, but he would never cease crowing over the fact that for all my study and Latin I was ending up as an innkeeper in Nimikon. That wouldn't do at all and so I am gradually beginning to await the old man's departure from this life, not with impatience but because the cause is a good one.

Recently, after long years of quiescence, Uncle Konrad has become involved in a fever of activity; I don't like the look of it. He goes about with his finger stuck perpetually in his mouth and his brow wrinkled with thought, strides round the room with rapid steps and when the weather is good, stares into space across the water. 'I think he has a mind to build boats again,' remarked old Cenzine, and in fact he certainly looks more animated and defiant than he has for years. He wears a knowing and superior expression on his face as if he knew exactly what he was about this time. But I do not think he really means business, it is merely a weary soul longing for wings to take his homeward flight. Uncle Konrad will certainly have to take sails with him. When it finally comes to that, the inhabitants of Nimikon are going to have an extraordinary experience for I have decided that when the pastor has finished I myself shall pronounce a few words by his graveside – which will be an unheard of thing in these parts. I intend to eulogise my uncle as a blessed and beloved son of God, which edifying speech will be followed by a nice sprinkling of pointed remarks for the benefit of the mourners who will be in no hurry to forget or forgive them. I hope my father will survive to witness this occasion.

The beginning of my great poetic composition still lies in the drawer. 'My Life's Work' I might call it, if it didn't sound too pretentious. But I would do well to keep quiet about it, for the poor thing, I must confess, is weak on its pins and unlikely to get far or reach a conclusion. Perhaps a time will come when I shall start on it again and see it through to the end. It would be the fulfilment of a youthful ambition and a proof that I am a writer after all.

This would be as important to me, if not more so, than the parish council and the stone-facings of the river bank. All the same it would not mean as much as the things now past but of permanent worth, the memories of all the people that have a place in my heart, from slender Rösi Girtanner to poor Boppi.

More about Penguins and Pelicans

Penguinews, which appears every month, contains details of all the new books issued by Penguins as they are published. From time to time it is supplemented by *Penguins in Print*, which is a complete list of all available books published by Penguins. (There are well over four thousand of these.)

A specimen copy of *Penguinews* will be sent to you free on request. For a year's issues (including the complete lists) please send 30p if you live in the United Kingdom, or 60p if you live elsewhere. Just write to Dept EP, Penguin Books Ltd, Harmondsworth, Middlesex, enclosing a cheque or postal order, and your name will be added to the mailing list.

Note: *Penguinews* and *Penguins in Print* are not available in the U.S.A. or Canada

Hermann Hesse

Herman Hesse (1877 – 1962), novelist and poet, won many
literary awards including the Nobel prize (1946). He was
interested in both psychology and Indian mysticism and
his novels explore different attempts to find a 'total
reality' in life.

The Glass Bead Game

The Glass Bead Game is an ultra-aesthetic game which is
played by the scholars, creamed off in childhood and
nurtured in élite schools, in the kingdom of Castalia.

The Master of the Glass Bead Game, Joseph Knecht,
holds the most exalted office in Castalia. He personifies
the detachment, serenity, and aesthetic vision which
rewards a life dedicated to perfection of the intellect.

But can, indeed, should man live isolated from hunger,
family, children, women, in a perfect world where
passions are tamed by meditation, where academic
discipline and order are paramount?

This is Hermann Hesse's great novel. It is a major
contribution to contemporary philosophic literature and has
a powerful vision of universality, the inner unity of man's
cultural ideals, and his search for personal perfection and
social responsibillity.

Also available
Steppenwolf
Narziss and Goldmund

Not for sale in the U.S.A.

Hermann Hesse

Gertrude

In this novel about the destructive nature of love, the central theme is the narrator's enduring and hopeless passion for Gertrude whom he meets through their mutual love of music. When Gertrude marries his friend, a famous singer, he watches passively while they slowly destroy each other – a destruction which culminates in the singer's tragic suicide. Hesse with his customary insight and penetration traces the effects of unrequited love on the emotional development of a sensitive young composer.

'It would be a pity to miss this book - it has such a rare flavour of truth and simplicity.' – Stevie Smith in the *Observer*.

Also available
The Prodigy

Not for sale in the U.S.A.